"Varga offers up a moral tale featuring a vivid cast, most notably a pair of down-and-out grave robbers. The story is told through Sheriff Sam Carter, who regards himself as a plain and simple lawman, interested only in the facts. But as he peers ever deeper into the peculiar case at hand, he finds himself asking questions neither plain nor simple concerning the true nature of Justice. A compelling read."

—JOHN MANDERINO,
author of *Bopper's Progress*

"It's not often that one finds a novel that simultaneously evokes smiles and tears. . . . This book, told from a lawman's somewhat limited perspective, has great plot twists with insightful investigation and courtroom scenes, as well as snappy and thoughtful dialogue throughout. I highly recommend this book."

—RENA MARIE VAN TINE,
past president, the Asian American Bar Association—Chicago

"In a style evocative of Harper Lee's *To Kill a Mockingbird*, James Varga's *Tombs of Little Egypt* tackles a timeless array of personal and professional moral issues. Set in the South and told from the perspective of a small-town sheriff, the novel offers an engaging plot punctuated by common sense and uncommon wisdom. Until the very end, there is uncertainty about whether a small community can do justice to strangers accused of hideous crimes."

—VINCENT R. JOHNSON,
St. Mary's University School of Law

"Jim Varga has shown that he is a very capable storyteller, combining a rural town of intriguing yet very ordinary characters with local politics and a court system ambivalent to change. It is a very readable story, at times mixing human tragedy with people who come alive to restore your faith. . . . Very enjoyable! If you put it down, the characters will still be running through your head."

—TERRY SULLIVAN,
Killer Clown: The John Wayne Gacy Murders

Tombs of Little Egypt

Tombs of Little Egypt

A Novel

James Varga

RESOURCE *Publications* · Eugene, Oregon

TOMBS OF LITTLE EGYPT
A Novel

Resource Publications
An Imprint of Wipf and Stock Publishers
199 W. 8th Ave., Suite 3
Eugene, OR 97401

www.wipfandstock.com

PAPERBACK ISBN: 978-1-6667-3858-2
HARDCOVER ISBN: 978-1-6667-9947-7
EBOOK ISBN: 978-1-6667-9948-4

SEPTEMBER 23, 2024 9:53 AM

This is a work of literary fiction. The story refers to historical facts (names, places, and events) and also small cities that still exist today. The main characters and locations in the story, their names, and incidents are products of the author's imagination or are used fictitiously. Any resemblance to actual persons, living or dead, places, or events is entirely coincidental and not intended by the author. Greens Point and Clermont County, Illinois, do not exist.

To Nancy and our children: Sam, Hannah, Ben, and Victoria

Chapter 1

"Y ou're on the wrong side," I said to both heroes of history, joking to myself.

In the center of our town square, a lawn and bushes surround a round granite water fountain. Across from each other stand two statues of Civil War heroes from Little Egypt: Thorndike Brooks and Green Berry Raum. The great debate or great debacle—and I'm not talking about the war that tore our nation asunder—is why they stand where they have stood for all of these years. History is silent on the matter. Rumor, the second cousin of history, has it that the two spots where they were christened were chosen either intentionally for some unknown reason, including a joke, or unintentionally. That's not saying much but does cover all the bases. The park ends Main Street, which was built from east to west on a straight line that runs along latitude 37° 9' 12" N, according to our local historian.

Standing erect on the south side of the fountain is Green Berry Raum, a brigadier general in the Union Army, who later became a U.S. representative and an IRS commissioner. He was from Golconda, our neighboring town along the Ohio River. Back-to-back but on the north side, across the sliding sheet of water dripping off the round fountain, is Thorndike Brooks, who took over a couple dozen residents of Marion and formed Company G, known as the Southern Illinois Company, of the Fifteenth Tennessee Regiment Volunteer Infantry of the Confederate Army. He became the highest-ranking Illinois resident to fight for the Confederacy. As lieutenant colonel, he was the only Southern Illinois rebel to make it to the end of the war and was present at the surrender of the Confederate Army of Tennessee in Durham (formerly Durham Station), North Carolina. Marion is northwest of the Ohio River next to Carbondale, now known for Southern

Illinois University. Few know that rebel sympathizers in Marion voted to succeed from the Union.

"It's not a joke until somebody laughs," Wally snorted, shots of spray sputtering from his lips. Too late, he slid a red-and-white paisley hanky back into a side pocket of his overalls. His white undershirt pressed out between the buttons on his blue-and-gray plaid shirt. Wallace Davis had me by a couple decades. He'd sit on one of the benches by the fountain and answer questions about the town. Because of his age, we believed some of his history, as he related firsthand accounts. The rest made us laugh. Who knew what stuff his stories were made of? The twinkle in his eyes kept his audience on their toes.

"Why do you think the South and the North swapped spots on our town square?" he whispered with a wink.

"That's what I came to ask you," I answered.

"You go find out. You're the sheriff, aren't you?"

I didn't need to answer our town's self-appointed historian, standing before him in my tan uniform and brass badge pinned on my chest. He waved me along, and I was much obliged to get on with my stroll up and down Main Street. I walked away and looked over my shoulder. He was beaming and waving over two little children, a boy and girl, and their mother. I sure hoped the two weren't going to ask him for help with their history homework.

✵ ✵ ✵

If possible, sleep on it. That's been my rule of thumb. I avoid snap decisions. In fact, the bigger the problem, the longer I hold back making up my mind. If I wait long enough, the problem seems to solve itself. I find that funny, but nine times out of ten it works.

I just don't know what I'd do if I couldn't let problems work themselves out. I was once in Chicago while on leave from the service. From what I recall, everything had to be done at once. Everybody was in a real hurry. From what I hear, things have just gotten worse. I don't have to return and get pushed about to find out if things slowed up there. I have a television to show me what I don't have to see for myself. Just last year, a jury in Chicago sentenced the serial killer John Wayne Gacy to death.

I'm Sam Carter. For twelve years, I was the sheriff of Clermont County. Before that, I was a deputy sheriff for another eighteen years. After thirty years of public service to the people of Clermont County, Illinois, I decided to pull off my badge, hang up my uniform, and retire from public life.

Greens Point, the county seat, is tucked up along a northern bend in the Ohio River. The southernmost part of Illinois is called Little Egypt because of its resemblance to the Nile Delta of Egypt. The Ohio River meets the Mississippi River downstream at Cairo, on the southern tip of Illinois. In Cairo, sandbagging against spring floods has grown to be an accepted and expected town activity.

The name Little Egypt could also have come from the Winter of Deep Snow in the 1830s that ruined crops and drove the Northerners south to the Carbondale region to buy grain, like the famine forced the sons of Jacob to Egypt for food during biblical times. Like a patchwork of homemade quilts, fields of grain stretch among the rivers, lakes, woods, and hills in Southern Illinois.

Towns throughout Southern Illinois stake their claims to the lore of Little Egypt. That's not to say Southern Illinois is Little Egypt. It's not. Where the line is drawn between the two depends on who's drawing the line. The folks in Salem, a city up north, parallel to St. Louis, call their city the "Gateway of Little Egypt" and sponsor an annual Little Egypt Festival. Legend links their region to a drought in the northern and central parts of our state in the 1820s that drove Northerners south for Salem's grain.

Another "Gateway of Little Egypt" is Centralia, home of the historic Sentinel building. Two colorful pharaoh head plaques adorn the main entrance to the headquarters of the *Centralia Evening Sentinel* and *Sunday Sentinel*, once proclaimed "Egypt's Greatest Daily." The Cahokia Mounds stand across the Mississippi River from St. Louis. The tallest mound, Monks Mound, rises up one hundred feet. A prehistoric native civilization built the mounds. Nevertheless, the earthen mounds can resemble the Egyptian pyramids, if a tourist or visitor looks really hard. Edwardsville was originally called Goshen by the early settlers, possibly from a resemblance to the land of Goshen in Egypt settled by the sons of Jacob, as recorded in the book of Genesis. Businesses slap the name Little Egypt onto their goods and services in an unwavering yet unsworn allegiance to the rural royalty.

The legend and lore go on and on.

Although Southern Illinois starts around Effingham, where hills begin to roll, I believe Little Egypt is much smaller and farther south. By the southernmost part of Illinois, I mean south from where the Wabash and Ohio Rivers meet on the southeastern border of our state. Geographically, the university's Saluki mascot and the *Daily Egyptian* newspaper just make the cut. From a different viewpoint, I would definitely include the bottom eleven counties, at most, the bottom sixteen to seventeen. With Greens Point pinned on the Ohio River, the townsfolk can rightfully claim their heritage to the title Little Egypt.

Over a century ago, Greens Point was a beehive buzzing with excitement. On top of being the county seat, she was the port town for the southeastern part of the state. All day long, barges hauled out piles of grain and coal to the rest of the country. Banks and businesses lined Main Street. At night, the money kept flowing, but the current directed it into saloons and dance halls. The sheriff and his deputies kept pretty busy with thieves, mostly, and maybe a stabbing in a back alley or down by the docks. Life was too fast for some, even back then.

Trucks, trains, and planes passed over the mighty Ohio and passed by Greens Point too. The flow of money shrank with the fall in riverboat traffic. The young folk followed the money in the trucks, trains, and planes. Our town grew old. The county seat became a sleepy little country town, rich in memories of its golden days.

As the sheriff for three terms, I could let problems work themselves out in the slumber years of the county. I always figured that, if a problem could work itself out alone over time, there was no need to interfere. Interference by me would bring in a second problem. Even with my deputy sheriffs, I didn't have the manpower to handle double trouble.

My job was to preserve law and order throughout the county. If I could sit in my office all day long without receiving a telephone call reporting a disturbance, then law and order was preserved, and I had done my duty. Not to take my job sitting down, I took my duty a step further. After lunch, I'd stroll up and down Main Street, greeting the public, to fulfill my duty as an elected official and digest my lunch.

With three successive quiet terms of office under my belt, little did I expect that Clermont County was suddenly going to awake. My telephone started ringing, and I found myself driving to every graveyard throughout the county.

Out of all this investigation and fuss, I decided to write a plain and simple account of the events from my last year as sheriff. My account contains no big-city psychology. I don't pretend to know the reasons for anybody's conduct. I also didn't include any morals-preaching. I confess that I'm not good enough for that. I chose to write this chronicle simply to set the record straight by telling what really happened down here in Greens Point.

✳ ✳ ✳

I stepped out of Tucker's Bar and Grill into a downpour. Every Friday, I stopped at Tucker's after work for dinner. That Friday, I ate liver and onions and drank a couple beers. The sound of the rain hitting the windows forced me to have a shot of bourbon before I left.

Tucker and I go back years. We both settled in Greens Point after we were discharged from the service. He'd been a cook in the service. He helped out the former owner of the bar and grill, who retired and sold the place to him. I landed a job as deputy sheriff. I'm sure my military background helped me get the job. I did, however, know a few people around town. My grandfather was once the mayor.

I drove down Main Street, not seeing a soul outside. Main Street runs over a block long. Along each side, shops like the bar and grill, the general store, the savings and loan, and my office stand. A few of the buildings have stood since the 1800s. The rain was falling mighty hard, but most of our residents go home on Friday nights. Greens Point is a family town.

A mile outside of town, on my way home, a wooden bridge runs over Bender's Creek. I slowed down the squad car to cross the bridge. The night outside of town was as dark as the inside of a cow. Clermont County doesn't have many highway lights or even highways. The county towns are connected mostly by country roads. Some of the roads out in the farmland aren't paved.

That's not altogether bad. The roads serve the county fine. People here don't do things just to be doing something or to be keeping up with the times. Besides, nobody knows where the times would take the county.

My headlights flashed on an old rusty pickup truck off to the side of the road across the bridge. I figured the truck had stalled in the rain and was abandoned. At least, I was hoping so.

As long as I can remember, I was never lucky. I drove over the bridge and parked in front of the truck. I pulled up the hood of my jacket and climbed out into the rain. As I walked back alongside the truck bed, I saw a pile of tools. In particular, I noticed a shovel covered with mud. I found none of the wheels stuck in the mud. By the rear of the truck, though, I saw footprints in the mud leading down under the bridge. Mud was splattered on some bushes, and a couple bushes had broken branches. I decided to see if the driver had taken refuge from the rain under the bridge. I walked down the slope and turned under the bridge.

"Howdy, there. Come on in out of the rain," a voice called out.

Two men were sitting by a campfire on top of the incline near the bottom of the bridge.

I started to walk over to the fire. "Are you two fellows stuck?" I asked.

"No, we ain't stuck," said the man who had greeted me.

I walked up to the fire.

"I'm Lou, and he's Duke," the man continued.

"Pleased to meet you. I'm Sheriff Carter. Can I help you?"

"No," answered Lou. "We're just taking a break. We've been on the road some time."

I saw an empty can of beans behind Duke. "There's a diner and motel in town," I told them.

"We're not much for towns," Lou said.

"Yep, we don't like towns, do we, Lou?" said Duke.

"That's what I told the sheriff, Duke. We like to keep to ourselves."

Duke wore a big smile on his face. Lou wore a slight grin. Duke looked huge. He looked to be maybe a half foot taller than me, and I was one of the tallest men in town. Whereas I was on the slim side, he had big bones. He had short, wiry hair that looked dull red or brown. Freckles dotted his light-brown skin and ran over his cheekbones and the bridge of his nose. He was wearing a denim jacket and overalls full of mud. Lou looked short and skinny with black, curly hair. The bottom of his front left tooth was chipped, and his nasal bone buckled under the skin. He was a bit cleaner. He was wearing a plaid shirt buttoned up to his neck and tan pants with a rope for a belt. Both were soaked. Duke's muddy brown boots and Lou's torn shoes were sitting close to the fire.

"You fellows will be on your way in the morning now, won't you?"

"We're just passing through, Sheriff," answered Lou.

"We're just passing through," said Duke.

"Fine. You two try to dry out."

"Thanks," Lou said. "It was real nice of you to look out for us."

Duke was just nodding and smiling. He seemed to be enjoying the campfire, despite the rain.

I walked back to the car, climbed in, and drove off. I thought they were drifters down on their luck. There's a lot of those kinds along the Ohio

River. Clermont County sees them come and go, now and then. We don't pay them any special mind. The county isn't rich or poor. We all get by. They get by their own way. Lou and Duke were causing no harm under the bridge. My duty was to solve problems, not make them. If they could get a dry sleep under the bridge, so be it. Greens Point wasn't going to crumble.

After driving a couple more miles, I pulled into our driveway. The lights in the living room and kitchen were on. Betsy was home. I get a contented feeling pulling up to our home in the rain, seeing the lights on, and knowing it is warm and dry inside. We built a fine home. It wasn't huge, but it was comfortable and ours. We found peace here in Greens Point.

I opened the front door and walked into our parlor. She was sitting on the sofa reading the *Bugler*, the town newspaper.

"Hi, honey," I called out.

She smiled.

"Susan called. We just hung up."

Susan is our daughter. She got married and moved off to Effingham. She married a good man, a printer, and gave us a couple grandchildren. With Effingham about three hours north by car, Betsy and I still see them on occasion.

I hung up my rain jacket and poured myself a bourbon to take the chill out of my bones. I slipped on my pajamas, old red-and-green-plaid flannel robe, and slippers and took Betsy's usual spot on the sofa by the pole lamp. She had moved to the dining room table, where she had spread out sheet music. Under the dining room light, the red hue in her chestnut brown hair glistened. She plays the organ at church on Sundays.

"Susan said the boys are doing well in school," she chirped. Her hazel eyes sparkled.

"That doesn't surprise me any. Those boys put together both puzzles we gave them last Christmas in no time. That one of Mount Rushmore was really tricky too." I let go a chuckle and shook my head. "On my way home tonight, I found two men by the creek under the bridge," I said.

"You don't say."

"Yeah, they had a fire going. They said they were just passing through."

"Oh, on a night like this."

"Well, that old bridge was giving them good cover."

"It's a pity how some must still go without."

The *Bugler* is no elaborate big-city newspaper. It keeps us posted on town meetings, church functions, and sales at the general store and market.

It's local and small. Jessie Daniels, a young reporter fresh out of college, occasionally wrote an article outside of the normal lines, but most of the time there's nothing but the routine to print.

I once saw a Sunday issue of the *Tribune* from Chicago. That paper was too big. It would take an entire Sunday to read. I figured the paper was put out Saturday evening to give buyers a jump on reading it, so they could have part of Sunday to do something other than go to church, read the paper, and eat dinner.

I set aside the *Bugler* and set down my bourbon. I flicked on the radio and took out my pipe. I get my pipes and tobacco through a mail-order catalog. I get quality tobacco at a good price.

The radio is good. Most of the stations in the county play country music. That's easy, relaxing music. It helps groom good moods and thoughts. The announcer has been on for years. He's funny. He's like a best friend to all of us who listen to him.

I like to sit back, blow smoke, and think about things. I like to think about Betsy, our home, Susan, the grandchildren, the town, and the Ohio River, always rolling on year after year. Sometimes, I think the Ohio is like a friendly old grandfather to the towns along the banks. He has raised the towns, which have all, with his help, grown and gone separate ways. I think he's a happy old crow, for the most part, with the life he has fostered in his valley.

Chapter 2

AFTER an easy weekend in the garden, in my workshop, and on the porch, I drove back into town Monday morning. As I drove over the bridge, I thought of Lou and Duke. The pickup truck was gone, so I concluded they had gone on their way.

The next three weeks rocked the very foundation of Greens Point. At the outset, I considered keeping the discoveries secret. But Greens Point knows no secrets. I would have my hands full responding to the discoveries, let alone trying to cover them up. Betsy doesn't care much for hiding things from the town. I guess she was right, especially since the town was going to find out anyhow.

I received the first call the Friday after I met those two drifters under the bridge. I got the call over at Tucker's. It was Haney who called. I hadn't seen him for two to three months. "Sheriff Carter."

"Sam, it's me, Haney."

"Haney, how are you doing?"

"Sam, there's trouble out here. It's awful."

"Say that again."

"A grave's been dug up . . ."

"Do you know what you're saying?"

"I do know what I'm saying, and I'm saying a grave's been dug up. Can you come out here fast?"

"I'll be out there in an hour."

"Can't you make it faster?"

"I'll see what I can do."

"And Sam?"

"What?"

"Don't tell Tucker."

"I won't."

I handed the telephone back to Tucker, who was standing behind the bar.

Haney sounded rattled. He ran the cemetery just outside of town. After his call, I still didn't know what he was talking about. I didn't believe a word he had told me. He'd probably overreacted. I had my duty to the public, though, and the public had been good to me. I finished my dinner and ordered another beer. Since Tucker didn't seem too interested in the call, I didn't tell him about it. After I finished my beer, I drove out of town over Bender Creek Bridge a short distance to the gate at Holy Hill.

Holy Hill is our prettiest cemetery. A low white picket fence runs around it. The outside of the office looks like a cottage. The cemetery sits on top of a rise. Magnolia trees and southern pines dot the landscape. All of the landed gentry are buried there from days gone by. With the old money went the ornate headstones. Almost every kind of color and shape possible in marble is set over the graves.

My grandfather is buried there, along with all of the other past mayors of Greens Point. I believe there's little room left for my age group. Before the golden days of Greens Point passed, the plots pretty near filled up. Nowadays, folks kind of view Holy Hill as a historical site for the county. The old-timers left still sitting on the bench in front of Herman's barbershop could tell the history of Clermont County from the Civil War to the present just from reciting the headstones.

When I walked into the office and heard the bell jangle, I saw Haney come out from the back room without his suit coat. Nobody sees him without his full suit on. I began to take seriously what he had told me over the phone. He looked red and sweaty.

"Haney, what's going on out here?"

"It's awful, just awful. There's never been any foul play up on Holy Hill."

"Slow down. You've got the sheriff out here now and on Friday night. Let's ease back a bit. You can't have that big of a problem."

I took a hard look at him. He didn't look good. His eyes were bloodshot, but I didn't smell any booze on him. Not that he was known to drink to excess, but a man can drink to excess now and then. He was holding his belly bulging out between his black vest and big silver belt buckle. Sweat trickled down his temples from his greasy black hair. I measured up the problem to be mighty big and maybe serious. "Do you want to tell me again what you say you saw?"

"It was awful, Sam."

"I know that already. You told me that on the phone and as soon as I got here. You sit down over there by the lamp."

He flopped down on an overstuffed chair by a special owl lamp he used to always brag about. I never saw a lamp like it anywhere else. The base of the lamp was made of plaster of Paris and shaped like an owl, white and brown and three hands high, with brown reflector eyes. He was really proud of that lamp. "The only one of a kind," he used to say. He fell down into the chair as if he were trying to dump the world off of his shoulders. The reflector owl eyes were staring at him. That's the type of furniture not found in even the Sears or Wards catalogs. I never asked him where he found the lamp. The lamp wouldn't match Betsy's décor in the parlor.

"Let's back up and start a bit slower. Don't tell me right off what you found. Start by telling me how you found it."

He took a deep breath and nodded. When he raised his head, he started to tell me, oh-so-slowly.

"I was out making my spring check of the grounds, you know, just walking around the Hill, seeing if winter marked the Hill any, when I think I see some torn earth on the south rise. Mind you now, that lazy Norman never called my attention to it. I want you to interrogate him right away. He's broad backed. I never should have trusted that man. He has nothing worth losing to be honest."

"Hold it one minute. Don't you start pointing any fingers. That's my elected duty. I don't tell you where or how to dig graves."

He sighed and nodded. I had to grasp control of the situation.

"Like I was saying, I saw some earth torn up on the south rise, so I walked on over there. As I got closer, I kept seeing more and more and hoping more and more that I was mistaken, but I found out I wasn't."

I pulled up a chair in front of him. "So tell me, what did you see?"

"The grave was dug up."

I gave him a moment to adjust. Then I took a couple.

"I walked up to the grave and saw the coffin top split off," he gulped.

I gave us another moment, but that did no good. He was rattled. "Did you look inside?"

"Heck, no. I ran back to my car and flew back to the office. When I came to my senses, I felt I had to call you, to make a report or something."

"I'm glad you did. You did the right thing. Now, you just sit still awhile. Take a few deep breaths. Let me do some thinking."

A minute passed without anybody saying a word.

There wasn't much hard thinking for me to do under the circumstances. There was only one thing I could do. I tried to think up something else, but the answer was right there in front of me. I had to go out to inspect the grave.

When the decision sank in, I quickly glanced out of the window, even though I knew the sun had set. Of course, I wasn't scared to walk out in the graveyard at night, but I would have preferred to begin my official investigation the next day. "Haney?"

"Yeah, Sam?"

"I'm done thinking."

His body stiffened up. "Yeah, well, what do you suppose we ought to do?"

"Do you have a flashlight around here?"

"Sam."

"I have a duty to do. You know I have to investigate."

"Don't you think you're pushing it a mite too hard for the first night?"

I stood up. "You don't have to go back. You just tell me where I can find this dug-up grave."

He rubbed his whiskered jowls with his fat hand. "Nonsense. I suppose it's all right with the sheriff and all. You got your gun?"

I nodded and sent him an easy smile.

He shrugged his shoulders and walked in the back room. He returned and handed me a wide-mouthed flashlight. "If you say so."

We climbed into the squad car and drove to the south rise. The night was clear but damp. The tombstones shined white in the headlights. A weak creek cut through Holy Hill. The slopes down to the creek fell below the beams of the headlights and looked awfully black. Despite all of the years I lived in Greens Point, I first noticed that night that Holy Hill had no hill.

As we slowed down on our approach to the south rise, the sound of the crushed rocks beneath the tires grew louder. But for Haney's directions, we didn't talk.

Two grown men in a graveyard at night aren't particularly scared. Nevertheless, we weren't really keen on inspecting an open grave. A busted grave fell far beyond our southern sense of decency and pulled us into the unknown. Up until that night, I can honestly say I'd never peered into a dug-up grave. I don't think men, even the sheriff, are supposed to be snooping into graves, whatever the reason. I kept thinking maybe we needed a reverend or some holy man to accompany us for such a religious task. But by the time I turned off the engine, I figured it was too late to turn back. Try as I did, I couldn't think of anybody but the sheriff who was supposed to be doing the inspection. I didn't even look at Haney before I threw open my door. I picked up the flashlight and climbed out of the car.

A graveyard at night is darn quiet. The trunks and limbs of the trees seemed to me to be whispering in the gentle breeze. The beam of the flashlight came alive as I turned it loose to scan the gently rolling landscape. Haney still hadn't spoken. He just pointed, and we walked. The beam fell on a rough mound of black earth. Unintentionally, we both stopped for a few seconds before we plodded on. I thought of Betsy and what she would say. I supposed she would have sanctioned the inspection.

Slowly, we walked up to the mound. We stepped to the side of the mound. I sent the beam down into the pit. I felt I had to. The beam quivered as it rolled over the open coffin.

"Haney," I whispered.

"What?"

"How good are these batteries?"

"I don't know."

I was hoping he would have had a better answer. "The coffin's open."

"You didn't think I was fooling, did you?"

"Fooling, no. Maybe mistaken."

"Well, you saw it. How about if you write your report and finish your official inspection tomorrow?"

"I guess I could."

I let a few seconds pass. I shouldn't have, because I almost agreed to finish the inspection tomorrow. I took a deep breath. "Let's go."

With me being a military man and a lawman on top of that, I always felt an ingrained duty pushing me onward. Looking back, I didn't care too much for most of the places I was pushed. That night at Holy Hill was no exception.

I stepped closer to the pile of earth. I turned the flashlight over the open coffin, and the beam zoomed up to the treetops by itself. "Come over here, Haney. This is your graveyard."

"I only own it. Norman, he digs it."

"If you don't ease up, I'm going to appoint you deputy sheriff to this investigation and order you down into that grave."

He slid up behind me. But for a quick peek, he wasn't about to look.

I steadied the light on the treetops and pulled it slowly down to the coffin again.

I stared at the corpse a whole half minute before my mind began to register. A man's remains lay in the coffin. The head resembled a mummy. The flashlight highlighted the petrified flesh or tendons that clung onto the bone, but the light didn't penetrate the black sunken eye sockets. I didn't care to move closer to examine those eye pits. The thin hair looked brittle, like winter brush. He was wrapped in a decomposed brown wool suit. Bug larvae had feasted on it. In all, he appeared to be a pretty short fellow.

The longer I looked at him, the more I noticed some peculiarities. His suit coat was pulled to his sides, and all of his pockets were pulled out. He wasn't wearing a belt or shoes.

I decided to end the preliminary investigation. I turned and stepped on Haney's toes. He spun around and hopped beyond the dirt pile.

"That's one humbling sight," I mumbled to him.

"I figured as much. I wasn't about to look. I still have faith in the human race." He mumbled to himself. He was rattled and babbling nonsense.

"That corpse is rotten to the bone. You don't guarantee widows airtight boxes, do you?" I said, attempting to rescue us with humor.

"I'd have to check the serial number on the coffin and the grave site number," he replied earnestly.

I had thrown him a line, but he hadn't caught it.

"I can look it up for you, in case you want it for your official report," he continued.

"Forget it, Haney."

We slowly climbed back in the county squad car. I didn't even try to talk to him. He sat tight with his hands on his knees and his eyes staring straight ahead.

After ten minutes in the office, he began to loosen up a bit. He stood up from his overstuffed easy chair and poured a mug of coffee. "Do you want a cup, Sam?"

"I don't take a cup after lunch. Coffee keeps me up at night."

"There ain't no way I'm going to sleep tonight. You ain't going to tell anybody in town, are you?"

I've always found that the person who asks to keep a matter secret is the first person to talk. "I'm the sheriff, not a reporter for the *Bugler*. I'll have to write a report. I have my duty."

"Yeah, sure. I suppose you got to write a report."

Haney was sweating really bad. Drops of sweat, weighed down with hair oil, rolled down his forehead. He wiped his face with a big white hanky.

After he sat back in his easy chair with his mug of coffee, I began questioning. I tried to keep it easy on him. "Could you give me all your records on that grave by, say, tomorrow afternoon?"

"Sure."

I could tell he wasn't listening to me. "I'm hoping your records can shed some light on some peculiarities puzzling me."

"What did you see, Sam?"

I looked to see if he was sitting all right. "That corpse didn't have a belt or shoes," I told him.

"You don't say."

"Well now, I'm pretty sure. I didn't go and touch the corpse."

"What do you think? Grave robbers?" He asked. He was getting flustered again. "Grave robbers at this day and age?" he groped. His head flopped from side to hide, and he pressed his palm against his forehead. He squeezed his eyes shut. He was starting to run off on a tangent.

"A man could buy or steal a belt or shoes from a store," I broke in. "Let's hold off thinking until we do some more seeing."

He pondered his black coffee for a few seconds. "Norman." He broke from his trance. "I told you from the get-go, didn't I? He's been acting mighty funny the last couple of weeks."

"How does he regularly act?"

"Funny, come to think of it. But that still doesn't change my mind."

"I also think it's a bit too early to be finger-pointing."

"It all adds up."

"You hold off. I've talked to Norman now and then. He seems like a decent sort—not too bright, but not dishonest either. How's he been acting funny lately?"

"I haven't seen him the last couple of weeks."

"How's that?"

"I haven't seen him. That's funny."

"Have you had any burials for him to dig?"

"No."

"Well then."

"But he's got a back as broad as a mule's. He can dig graves and toss around caskets like nobody I ever saw. That's why I hired him."

"That's right. That's his job. Of course, he's good at it. A man doesn't suddenly risk losing his job that he's worked for years by stealing on his job. A man doesn't bite the hand that feeds him."

"What about Clara Jeffries catching Nell Woods lifting ten dollars from the cash register at the general store?"

"Hold on a second. That's going too far. Don't drag poor Nellie into this mess. Pete died. The kids had all moved away. She had a problem. She was more lonely than guilty. Besides, she got over all that. She's doing fine now."

"Problems? You think Norman ain't got problems? What man would dig graves for a living and live in a chicken coop on the outskirts of town?"

"A simple guy earning chicken feed for wages. Besides, you haven't had a burial in a year."

"It don't matter. He cuts the grass and trims the bushes." Haney rustled back in his easy chair.

Shortly afterwards, I left Holy Hill. By the time I got home, Betsy was off the sofa, out of the front room, and sitting on our bed in her robe. "How'd the day go?" she asked.

"A might hard," I replied.

After I took off my uniform and slipped into my pajamas, I sat on the edge of our bed and told her what I had seen. She nodded. That didn't surprise me. She comes from a strong family stock. Her family stretches back almost to the Mayflower. I've never been able to trace my family beyond Clermont County.

Chapter 3

I LIKE my eggs fried crisply around the edge and my bacon chewy. We hardly talked through breakfast. Betsy asked me how I was feeling. I told her, tired. Every change in seasons, I grow sleepy—so I told her. She didn't ask questions for answers she knew she wouldn't like. She nodded, but she knew. I knew that she knew, but I just nodded in return.

Sometimes, life is one head nod after another. In Greens Point, we have certain manners. We know a head nod means more than agreement. More often than not, a head nod means, "I see what you're saying or I don't believe you, but I'd rather not talk about it right now." As I said, Betsy knew.

After breakfast, I drove into town. For most of the way, I thought about the previous night. I then began to plan my day. First, I'd get my daily duties out of the way. Second, I'd pick up the records from Haney. Third, I'd talk to Norman. Last, armed with the records and my interview of my only suspect, if he was even that, I'd make my final inspection before laying the body back to rest. I didn't want to start the day peering into a grave at some corpse. Duty continues, but execution can vary.

I drove straight to my office on Main Street. After thinking about Holy Hill during most of the drive and having already planned my day, I decided that I could take a break. I made a pot of coffee and spread out the *Bugler* on my desk to relax a half hour. I was glad to have the office to myself.

Pursuant to my official duties, I made my daily rounds in the office. I walked to the empty cells in the back room to see if the beds were made, looked in the bathroom to see if there were enough paper hand towels and toilet paper, and checked the wastepaper basket behind my desk to see if the basket needed to be emptied out back.

As usual, all was in proper order. Old Jeb was good at his duties. Since crime was running low during my terms, as it had for over half a century, I focused my energies on order, not to mention my public access during my post-lunch strolls up and down Main Street.

Still executing my public duties, I read through my mail. I sipped on a cup of freshly brewed coffee. There's something satisfying about drinking fresh hot coffee alone. I had a keen display of those black-and-white wanted-persons posters thumbtacked to my corkboard on the wall. All the kids in town loved to look at the faces. I combed through my mail each morning for more photographs for my collection.

That morning, I received in the mail my magazine from the Fraternal Order of Police. That issue contained a lengthy article on lie detectors with all sorts of charts, graphs, and footnotes. I studied the article, looked at the charts and diagrams, and ignored the footnotes. At least, the charts and diagrams looked nice and were fun to figure out.

More often than not, after I figure out charts and diagrams, I don't believe them. I never trusted numbers. And I still don't understand the need for footnotes. If the information in the footnote is important, it should be in the text. If it isn't important, it shouldn't even be in a footnote. Endnotes are worse. They make reading more troublesome, following the numbers here and there to this page and that page. I think writers use footnotes to appear intelligent. I haven't used a single footnote or endnote throughout my entire story.

I left the magazine out on my desk, so Hank would see it. Being as hard-charging as he was, he stayed on top of all new developments, regardless of their need.

By the time I executed my morning duties, lunchtime arrived. I learned a long time ago to space out work. If a person has to run a lifetime, there's no sense running at full throttle every day. The mind is just a muscle. It's got to be relaxed regularly, for maximum strength when it's needed.

I took out my sandwich. I was glad to see that homemade pot roast with lots of ketchup on white bread. The ketchup was pushing through the holes in the bread. It was dripping out of the sides of the sandwich. Betsy had cut the pot roast thick.

By the time I finished my sandwich, I had to begin my official walk up and down Main Street. As I said before, I was a man of duty. I was an elected official and owed the public. Whether I felt like it or not, I would walk up and down Main Street every day unless a hard rain or heavy snow was falling. When the weather was so harsh, I stayed in the office. Nevertheless, I carried out my duty. There wasn't anybody on the street anyway in a storm.

I had a fine walk after my pot roast sandwich. Looking back, I think spring might have woken up the town. I saw Tess Springer, Bea Ferguson, Helen Turner, Frank Buckhorn, and Tommy Sparks. Not one of them was sullen. On the contrary, everybody was happy. There was an easy breeze drifting up Main Street. A southern breeze carried up to the town the fresh, sweet smell of those baby buds of flowers and leaves opening up along the Ohio River. Halfway up my walk, I figured Haney had kept his mouth shut so far. Of course, I figured he had to stay shut up. His livelihood kept him shut up.

Tess Springer was a tall, slender woman with probably more gray hair than brown. Her eyeglasses made her eyes look twice as big as they were. I asked her how Don was doing, and I think she gave me the answer she gives to me every spring: "Don's riding as tall in the cab as when I married him." The cab Tess spoke of was the tractor cab on their farm. Of course, Don was riding more sunken with age each year. That darn answer, though—it was typical in Greens Point. We were all proud and lied whenever we could to protect ourselves. Since everybody knew his or her neighbor was lying, nobody took offense. We lied in good faith.

Bea Ferguson, God bless her soul, was the opposite of Tess. She was heavyset and walked with a limp to the left. She claimed she had a bad ankle. I believe she just weighed a might too much for her two ankles. Bea was married to Burt, the town plumber. They were well off, with all of the old buildings around the county. To hear Bea tell it, I don't think any outsider would know that their money shored up the savings and loan. Vic Bottoms, the president of the savings and loan, would just smile at the sound of the Fergusons' name. Beneath his long, thin nose, his smile would spread out broader than his skinny frame. Vic had the lightest blue eyes in town. His smile, or their deposits, lit up those blue eyes.

Helen Turner and Frank Buckhorn were all right in my book. Every sheriff understood residents like them: they were neither good nor bad, for the most part. They had problems. Frank drank a bit too much on the weekends. Regardless, he was the handiest man in Greens Point, including Burt. Burt didn't care for Frank. There was nothing around the house that Frank couldn't fix. He never took money. Folks knew a drink would please him. He'd work all day Saturday and be pleased with a few drinks.

The drinks never pleased Margaret, his wife, but she was a saint. Nobody ever saw her. She kept at home. A tornado couldn't sweep Margaret out of her home. For every kind of collection, Margaret would pitch in a dollar or two. She was that silent, pure type. She did more quietly than a pastor could from the pulpit.

Helen Turner, no relation to my deputy, was a widow and getting up in years, but she had the church. Helen lived alone and showed no signs of wanting anybody's attention, except for her occasionally talking to herself when she thought nobody was around.

Tommy Sparks was something else. He was the mechanic at the corner gas station. The best thing that could be said about Tommy was that he was still young and had a few more years to grow up. I knew Tommy when he was just a boy. He had a foul mouth and still does.

I locked him up a few times, not because he was mean but on account of his mouth. He popped off too much. After he slept off his whiskey, he was apologetic.

On the weekends, Tommy could be found at the bar more often than Tucker. He was single and needed a wife badly. In a family town like Greens Point, he couldn't be faulted too much for his drinking and carrying on. I always figured, in a couple years, he'd settle down and have a family to account for. I'd been figuring so for quite some years, without any prospects in sight. Regardless, he was a good mechanic. He serviced the county cars.

After my rounds, I drove over to Holy Hill to check in on Haney. He looked bad. He had lost that nervous energy and had sunk to rejection. He hadn't shaved and was wearing the same black vest he'd had on last night.

He was sitting behind his big old desk when I walked into the office. As soon as he saw me, he reached for some papers. "Here are the records. They ain't much, but I hope they'll help you some."

He handed me a couple sheets of paper. The paper didn't look that old. The ink was dark enough to have been written last night. Still, I thanked him for his help and sat down to study the papers.

From the papers, I learned that the corpse was one Henry Albrecht. He was buried August 9, 1884. He had passed after Marianne, his wife, who was buried next to him. Anybody investigating the occurrence could have learned the above facts and the remaining facts on the papers from a mere reading of the headstones.

"Is this all you have?"

"That's it. I hope it helps you."

I shook my head. "Can I take these?"

He nodded.

"I'll return them."

He nodded.

"Lay off the coffee and get some sleep, would you?"

"I ran out of coffee."

I left the office, climbed into the squad car, and drove out of the cemetery to an old farm a few miles out of town. Along the way, I drove through some of the prettiest country in the county. Along the Ohio River Valley, creeks splash down to the river, and trees and bushes swell up in the rich black soil.

I drove up to a farm set up on another rise from the drain to the river. The acreage was prime farmland but totally neglected. Most of the acreage was left wild. The farm was owned by Muriel Horner. Joe died ten years ago.

There was a faded white farmhouse behind a whitewashed fence running along the road. A few magnolias dotted the yard.

Magnolias are Southern Illinois. Early in spring, the winding gray boughs bear the large white-and-pink flowers. The flowers cast off a heavy, sweet scent. Springtime is marked by the sleepy magnolia scent. As summer approaches, the flowers grow brown and fall from the boughs, and the sweet scent grows stale. As the years have passed, I've come to look forward to the magnolia flowers each spring.

On the front door of a farmhouse, I've learned that it is necessary to bang hard. A tarnished brass knocker dimly glistened in the center of the door. Instead, I rapped on the small window set up too high on the wooden door for poor little Muriel to look through. I waited and rapped again, but this time with the wedding ring. I waited another half minute. I heard motion in the house, and the door slowly opened.

"Why, Sam, what brings you out this way?" Muriel asked.

"A good spring day."

I hadn't seen Muriel in about a year. In that short time span, she appeared to have grown much older. Whereas my hair had become sprinkled with white, her hair was a dull gray. She was wearing a plain brown dress wrapped in a loose navy blue sweater.

"How's the farm, Muriel?"

"No changes here. Nothing ever changes here on the farm."

We paused.

"Lord's sake. Where are my manners? You come on in here. Have you eaten lunch? I've got some pot roast left over."

"Oh, no. I've eaten. Betsy fixed me a pot roast sandwich for lunch."

I stepped inside the farmhouse and smelled that dusty smell of old forgotten homes. She ushered me to the kitchen filled with the aroma of fresh coffee. The percolator popped coffee that grew darker. From the windows on the rear door and a window over the sink, the kitchen seemed to be the brightest room in the house. For some reason I couldn't put my finger on, I was glad.

After a little small talk, I asked Muriel about Norman. She told me that, if he wasn't in the barn with the cows or in the pig pen, he might be in his room next to the barn. She began to tell me where the pen was, when I told her I still remembered where it was. That brought a smile to her face. Somebody remembered. That must have brought on memories of the old days with Joe. I felt glad to have brought a smile on her face. Old folks don't need any more pain.

I walked from the back porch about twenty yards to the old peeling barn. I walked around to the side of the barn by the maple trees. As I neared the corner of the barn, I heard a harmonica whining lazily. Attached to the barn stood a whitewashed shed beneath the maple trees. At the door of this shed, I saw some rocks spread around the door to look like a porch. The harmonica stopped. Norman opened the door.

Damn, he was huge. He was almost as wide and tall as the doorway. When he saw me, his dark face twitched half surprise and half concern. That look didn't sit too well with me. At that point in the investigation, I was the only one in his corner.

"Sheriff Sam. What you doin' here?"

"Don't stop playing on account of me."

"I was only messin'. What do you want?"

We were still standing on his rock porch. He didn't know what do.

"Do you mind if I come in for a bit?"

"Uh, sure. I ain't got nothin', though."

He was now smiling ear to ear. I was glad to see that innocent smile.

I stepped into a one-room shed. There was a woodburning stove at one end and a table and chair at the other. Opposite the door was a small cot for the huge man. Next to the doorway, there was a collection of books. He had wedged scores of books, mostly paperbacks, on wooden boards stacked on cement blocks.

"Have you read all of these?"

"Some. I can't get through most."

"Let me see here. Mark Twain—"

"Yep, I like books that tell stories."

"How about music?"

"Yep, I like music too."

"From what I heard, you play pretty good."

He smiled and cast his eyes and head down.

I stepped closer to the table to take a better look at his harmonica, but he stepped over and grabbed it.

"It's just an old thin," he said, as he stuffed it into his pants pocket. He looked down at the floor. The floorboards were covered with a threadbare rug, probably an old one from the farmhouse.

"What have you been doing lately, Norman?"

His eyes flashed up into mine for a split second, then flashed off around the room. I looked around his room again. His simple place was neat and clean. His old leather boots, though worn, hadn't a trace of mud on them.

"I've been feedin' and milkin' the cows. I help Mrs. Horner with the chores."

"That's good of you."

"She's a good lady. She gave me a half cake just yesterday. She treats me real good here on the farm."

"She's lucky to have you out here to help her."

He smiled. "I do what I can."

"Say, Norman—"

His eyes flashed up again for a second.

"How's work been at Holy Hill?"

"Slow, but for the cuttin' and trimmin'. There's been no other need for me. Mr. Haney don't like me hangin' 'round the office."

"How about at night?"

"Night? No. I don't go there at night."

"Have you seen anybody pass by down the road to the cemetery?"

"That neither."

I stepped back to the door. "Do you work for Mr. Haney in those boots?"

"Sometimes. I got rubber boots for the mud. Those boots are outside on this side." He pointed to his left. "They're dryin'. I hosed them down this mornin'."

"Why?" I gave him a hard look.

"I had nothin' else to do, so I cleaned up 'round here."

I stepped out the door.

"Sheriff Sam, do you got a problem?"

"I'm not exactly sure yet. Do you mind if I look at those boots as I leave?"

"No, they're out there where I told you. Over there." He pointed to his left again.

"Thanks, Norman."

"Thank you for stoppin' in."

I turned around the corner of the shed. I saw a pair of clean tall black rubber boots. On my way to the squad car, he was standing in the doorway.

"By the way," I called out over my shoulder, "can you meet me at Haney's office in an hour?"

"Yes, sir. I'll be there in an hour."

I waved to Muriel, who was looking through the kitchen window, and climbed back into the county car. On the drive back, I felt about as ready as I ever would—not much. I pulled into Holy Hill and up before Haney's cottage.

Inside, he was sound asleep on his torn overstuffed chair. The jangling bell on the door did no good. He still hadn't changed. He looked like he'd been on a weeklong binge.

"Haney."

He rustled and began to focus.

"I'm going back to the grave."

His head fell back against the easy chair.

"You can wait here. I'll be back shortly."

Before closing the door, I called back to him. "Norman will be here in an hour."

He rolled his head back and forth. His eyes were still shut.

Funny, the daylight seemed to ease the walk to the grave considerably. The day didn't hide the graveyard like the night did. I guess I caught the jitters the night before from not clearly seeing what was out there, or so I thought, until I came up to that mound of earth on the south rise and had to look at what was down there.

Nobody ever ought to see a grave that's been dug up. My stomach turned inside out. A shiver shook my entire body. That body rotted into mostly bone. Petrified flesh or tendons clung onto the skull. The sunken eye sockets were black, as was the pit under the nose bone. The lips were peeled back from yellow and brown teeth. After one quick glance, I kept my eyes away from that face.

The pockets of the decomposed brown suit were turned out. I didn't see a belt or shoes. I pulled out my pencil and pad to jot down these clues.

An elaborate coffin held the shrunken corpse. I noted some ornate wood carving and brass handlebars. The wood on the lid was split in two places. I jotted down these clues. Holy Hill must have made a killing on the deal.

I stepped closer to the headstone to see if I could discover more information on Henry Albrecht than that contained in Haney's records. I couldn't. The information was the same. The headstone, though, was the biggest on the south rise. The grave site was perched at the top of a slow long downgrade to the creek and was partially hidden from the road by the trunk of a big old oak tree. The south rise was one of the farthest points from the office. I jotted down these observations along with my clues.

I had seen enough. I pulled out my pocket camera, snapped some photographs, and walked back to the office. I didn't try to do any figuring. I didn't try to force any ideas along.

Time after time, I've seen a person force ideas onto a problem only to mess it up. Like I said at the beginning of my story, I prefer to let problems work themselves out. Most of the time, they will, if nobody meddles with them.

Facts speak, if a person has the patience to wait and listen long and hard. Sometimes, facts whisper. Sometimes, they scream. The best way to approach them is to sit by them for as long as it takes them to start talking. They talk when they will.

Facts always talk. Nobody can force them to speak. If a person acts too fast, more often than not, that person will be fooled. I prefer to wait for the whole story before deciding what to do. Patience has gotten me this far in life. At my age, I don't see any reason to change.

When I walked back inside the office, Haney was pacing in front of an empty coffee pot. "Sam, what are we going to do?"

"Buy some more coffee and make another pot."

"No, no. I mean Holy Hill."

"You stop worrying. You should go to bed."

"I suppose you're right. It's now in your hands. It's your job. Ain't that right?"

"That's right. You have your job, and I have mine."

"Did you talk to Norman?"

"Don't start up on Norman. I talked to him. He didn't see anything at all."

"That's not what I mean."

Haney began to pace back and forth between the easy chair and empty coffee pot. His protruding belly had pulled his shirt out of his pants. A brown coffee stain ran down the front of his white shirt through his open vest. His thin oily black hair was messed up. "Don't let him throw you. He might not look as sharp as me or you, but he's shrewd. He's got those wild instincts. He's dumb like a fox. You got to lock him up right away before he catches your scent and runs off."

"Who's going to rebury that body?"

Haney paused a moment to think it through. "I can't fire him now," he said.

"And I can't arrest him now. You just stop."

The office door opened, and Norman walked inside. "Hello, Sheriff Sam, Mr. Haney."

"Hello, Norman," I said.

Haney, without looking at Norman, just nodded and walked back to the empty coffee pot.

I turned toward Norman. "Haney is going to take a nap, and you and I have us a job to do."

"What kind of job?"

"I'll tell you on the way."

"Sheriff Sam, you got a problem, don't you?"

Haney glanced over his shoulder at me.

"I'll tell you about that, too, on the way."

Haney walked into his home in the back rooms, and Norman and I walked out of the office. Though I was taller than most of the men in Greens Point, Norman stood at least half a head taller than me. I could almost hide just by standing directly behind him.

"Where do you keep the shovels?"

"In the shed with the lawnmower."

We walked to a shed next to the garage behind the office. He reached under a torn shingle on the roof of the shed and pulled down a key for the padlock.

"Mr. Haney bought this lock for me when I started workin' for him. I had trouble rememberin' the numbers for the old lock." He smiled.

"A key is a lot faster anyway," I told him. "I don't like fooling around with numbers on my job either." I reached into my pocket and pulled out my key ring to show him.

"Keys are faster, ain't they, Sheriff Sam."

He pushed the door open, and we stepped into the shed. I was a might sorry to see that the size of the tool shed was almost the size of his shed on the Horner spread.

He grabbed a spade and turned.

"No, you grab me a shovel too. While you're at it, we better take that black-headed rubber mallet."

"If you say so. Here, you take my shovel. I'll use this old one."

After he locked up the shed and carefully slid the key under the same shingle, we turned to walk toward the graveyard.

"What's wrong, Sheriff Sam?"

"I can't say yet. But right now, you and I have to bury a coffin."

"Why didn't Mr. Haney tell me?"

"Well, how can I say this? There's a grave over on the south rise that's been dug up."

His eyebrows jumped up. He gave me a hard stare. "No."

"Yes. So, today, we have to bury it again."

"I'll do just what you tell me, but why?"

"I can't leave the grave torn up."

"No. Why is the grave torn up?"

"I don't know for sure. I have to warn you, Norman, the coffin is broken open."

His face curled up.

"Right. And that goes double for me. I think we both ought to keep our eyes on the coffin and off the corpse."

He nodded readily in agreement.

I walked slowly enough to let him lead. He walked straight to the south rise. But as we neared the south rise, the mound came into view, so there wasn't any need to let him lead farther. I hated to play tricks on such a simple fellow.

When we arrived at the grave, he stopped and looked at me. "Well, Sheriff?"

"Yes, I suppose we should get started."

"Ain't you forgettin' to deputize me?"

I reached up and gave my head a scratch on hearing that one. "I hadn't really thought of that, except the county doesn't have any extra funds to pay for an extra deputy."

"I don't need money. All you got to do is swear me in."

"All right. I'll swear you in, but only for the burial."

"I accept."

I had him raise his right hand and repeat an oath I solemnly concocted right there on the spot while I had my hand raised. It did me no harm and appeared to do him some good. After all, we were on an official investigation, and I did have the power and authority vested in me.

After the short ceremony, we got down to business, and he climbed down into the grave. He was more used to that line of work than I was.

The reburial was beyond foul, to border on sick. He climbed down into the grave to slide the coffin top aright and pound it down firm. As soon as he climbed out of the grave, we began flinging shovelfuls of dirt on top of the coffin. The heavy dirt slapped a really mournful rhythm on the coffin top. As the drumbeat faded, I began to ease up.

After the grave was completely filled, I leaned back on my shovel and took in a deep breath. Although I couldn't put my finger on the problem, I just didn't feel right with a coffin sitting out in the broad daylight like a gallon of milk used to sit out on a porch. Even though I go to church every Sunday, I still had the jitters.

We banged down hard on the dirt with the flat sides of our spades to flatten the mound over the grave. Each whack on the mound seemed to calm my jitters. By the time we finished, we were sweating like nobody's business. And I'll say straight away, the packing wasn't all that drained the sweat from us.

After we plugged Mr. Albrecht back up, Norman grabbed the shovel out of my hand. "What are you goin' to do now, Sheriff Sam?"

"Right now? I'm heading back to my office."

When we got back to Haney's office, Haney was gone. He was probably asleep behind the office in his home.

"Come on, Norman. I'll give you a ride to Mrs. Horner's."

"Thanks, but no, Sheriff Sam. I like to walk. I ain't in no rush. Besides, the sooner I get back home, the more time I got to do nothin'."

"Suit yourself. Thanks for helping me. I'll see to it that Haney pays you."

"Thank you. I never been a deputy before."

I climbed into the squad car and drove down the road back to town. I looked and saw him walking off deep in the brush. A silver sheen traced the big fellow's dark skin across the back of his neck and along his bare arms. Actually, it seemed to me that he wasn't even following a path. I figured, if anybody knew Holy Hill, he did. I hated registering such facts. With Haney after him so badly, I felt as if I had to stand in his corner. Regardless of my feelings, I had my official duties. Whether I liked it or not, there was nobody in Greens Point as good a suspect. Of course, I didn't tell Haney my thoughts. I hated to agree with him.

I drove back to the office. I had forgotten to turn off the coffee pot. I flipped the switch and tossed my notepad into the top drawer of my desk. I didn't want to start writing my official report that day. I preferred to let my impressions ferment a day in the back of my mind. Facts have to be gathered and stored. Some sort of framework has to be conceived to place them in.

I hated to think Haney was right, but my mind kept drifting off to grave robbing. I was having all sorts of problems adjusting to the thought. Maybe a hundred years ago, a sheriff could have jumped on the thought. Somehow, the twentieth century seemed too modern for such a crime. We have welfare. Besides welfare, there was still theft, burglary, and armed robbery.

In other words, I figured a man could get money all sorts of ways other than grave robbing. I was holding out for another answer. I was hoping time would let the problem solve itself. I sure didn't want to rush into any grave robbing investigation.

Chapter 4

THERE's one thing I never liked, and that's paperwork. I enlisted in the service and landed a job in the Clermont County Sheriff's Office to act and do, not read and write. I grow bored and impatient turning over forms and documents. But when duty calls, I try to act. For two to three afternoons, I turned and read document after document from the records of the town Baptist church, the county recorder of deeds, and the savings and loan.

After following a lead from a couple of the oldest senior citizens in Greens Point, I went to the record books to learn about Henry Albrecht. Haney's records told me as much as a quick glance at the headstone. Wally's tip proved worthless. Henry Albrecht had nothing to do with the inverted Civil War heroes guarding our town square.

Henry Albrecht was the founder and president of the savings and loan over a hundred years ago. Up until his retirement, he was at the pinnacle of Greens Point financial and social circles. He excelled in private enterprise and actively engaged in public functions.

The Albrecht Manor rested high on a bluff above the Ohio. The manor was noted for the huge front porch that swung around the front of the manor to small side porches that led up to the main front porch. Directly in front of the manor, the porch steps fanned out in an upside-down *v* formation. Magnolias blossomed about the front yard all the way to the white wooden fence that ran along a country road. The view from the front porch was said to be spectacular. The manor faced south, and the front yard dropped off to the Ohio. Legend has it, Henry Albrecht spent each Sunday evening watching the sunset over the tree-lined shore of Kentucky.

CHAPTER 4

The manor's gone now. It burnt down. Legend also has it that lightning took down the manor, an act of God that swept away the steamboat days and set the stage for the twentieth century and the world wars. Rumor has it, though, that a river bum, sleeping off a drunken stupor, let it take to flame after it had fallen abandoned and in disrepair.

In the old days, the lives of certain persons embodied the life of the entire town. Such was the life of Henry Albrecht and Greens Point. Marianne, Henry's wife, was a quiet Baptist from Kentucky. According to town talk, Henry built the manor to face Marianne's home state. Despite Marianne's high social position in Greens Point, little is known about her. She kept to the manor. Henry and Marianne had one child, a daughter named Penny. I could trace her only back to her return to Kentucky. Before the demise of the Albrechts and the manor, the Albrechts were one of the richest families throughout Clermont County and southeastern Illinois.

Outside of that posh history, I could find no other connection between Mr. Albrecht's past and the current problem, other than that suggested by the grandeur of the headstone. The headstone boasted wealth in its size and ornamentation. Money kept looming larger in my mind. No matter which way I turned my mind's eye, that disgusting conclusion kept haunting me. Unless a sudden surprise was soon to jump out at me, I was going to have to conclude that grave robbers dug up the Albrecht grave in search of any gold, silver, or jewelry buried with him. Regardless of the indications, I kept holding out for something else.

✳ ✳ ✳

Tommy Sparks had set out on another binge. Tucker called and told me Tommy was doing bad. Tucker wanted me—not Hank—over fast. I learned Tommy had busted out the front picture window with an empty bottle of sour mash whiskey. Tucker told me over the telephone that Tommy threw that bottle unprovoked.

At the outset, I knew Tommy threw the bottle, but I wasn't so sure Tucker hadn't irked Tommy some. Those two had run-ins about once a month from June to September. Nevertheless, there was nothing Tucker could say to Tommy to justify a broken picture window. I expected a steak sandwich and fries to be waiting for me after I locked the boy up for the night. Tucker was always grateful for my official assistance.

After the call, I walked over to Tucker's. The window was busted out. An empty bottle of sour mash was lying alongside the curb out in front. I collected the bottle for evidence.

When I stepped inside of Tucker's, I saw Tommy slumped over a corner table. He was nodding off. Tommy never caused me any trouble. I knew his father before he died, and Tommy knew I knew his father.

Being the Clermont County sheriff is not hard if the sheriff knows how to approach his job. We were all basically friends in Greens Point. We all had troubles now and then, some more often than others. From past meetings, Tommy and I had grown closer. His father had died four years earlier. Since his father's death, I had seen him pretty regularly.

I walked over to the corner table and sat. He didn't budge. I pushed back his chair with my shoe. His head slowly raised. His eyes weren't focused yet. When his eyes came across me, his head fell plunk down on his crossed arms.

"Tommy."

"Give me a couple minutes here, Sheriff."

"The way I'm beginning to see it, you've been here too long already. Let's go."

I stood and grabbed him by the arm. He pressed himself off of the table and wobbled back against the corner wall.

I led him out of the bar, knocking over only one chair along the way. Tucker rolled his eyes up toward the ceiling and shook his head. I knew that, if Tommy paid Tucker for the damage, Tucker would drop the charges. In Greens Point, businesses and I preferred to work out certain situations between ourselves, like that steak sandwich that would be waiting for me.

As Clermont County sheriff, I had experience with the court system. After years of inactivity in the courts, I can only conclude that courts just delay a large share of the disputes and prolong the aggravation along the way. This results in lawyers, like doctors, regulating the infliction of pain on the general public. Their control of pain gives them their supremacy over the rest of us. Even in Clermont County, courts crept a bit too slowly. With me knowing just about everybody, we almost always reached agreements to bypass the courts.

I led Tommy across the street and down a few buildings to my office. Hank looked up from one of his law enforcement journals and then set back to reading. Hank knew Tommy was drunk again. I lowered him down gently on the bunk in cell number one. Over at the hot plate, I put a mug of water on to boil. After the water came to a boil, I dropped in a beef bouillon cube and wrapped the mug with a couple of paper towels. I carried the mug back into the cell and set it down on the floor beside his bunk.

"Tommy, how are you feeling?"

"Awful."

"Can you open your eyes yet?"

"No."

"I set your soup down here on the floor by the bunk. Try to sip some when you're ready."

"Thanks, Sheriff. Beef?"

"Yeah, it's beef."

I always boiled up some beef bouillon for him when I locked him up. His father and I were good friends. No matter how drunk he was, I found that mug empty when I returned the next morning, even when he told me he didn't want any soup.

"Tommy?"

His head flopped over from facing the wall to facing my kneecaps. His eyes still hadn't opened.

"Where have you been the past couple of days?"

"Greens Point."

"I know that. You're in Greens Point now. What have you been doing?"

"I've been on a roll."

"What are you talking about?"

"There's no good or bad anymore."

"Stop it. You're talking nonsense."

"I can't keep it up anymore."

"Shut up. You're talking like a fool."

"I can't be anything but a fool, Sheriff. I'm rolling straight to Holy Hill."

I'm sure my eyes flashed open. "What's that about Holy Hill?"

"I've got nowhere else to go. We've all got to go."

"Have you been up there lately?"

"I don't know. Have I?"

"Do you recall being at Holy Hill?"

"The last place I remember is Tucker's. All the rest is a blur."

I pushed his head back toward the wall. "I'll see you tomorrow morning."

I turned and locked his cell. I locked the cell to protect Tommy from himself, not to prevent an escape. Even if he did escape, I could find him at home in the morning, sleeping off the sour mash.

I walked over to the front door.

"You're so kind to drunks that they're starting to look forward to spending the night here," Hank quipped.

"Hank," I called back, "you're not going to find any articles on decency in those journals. Lock up the office when you leave."

I returned to Tucker's for dinner. After his call asking for my assistance, I had put Betsy on notice that I would be late. There were just a couple of customers in Tucker's. I ate my dinner at the bar. I got the fries that I was expecting, but the steak sandwich had turned into a hamburger.

"So what went on between you and Tommy?" I asked Tucker.

"Nothing special. He got drunk on sour mash like he does every spring. I should have seen it coming. But you know Tommy. He's such an easygoing, likable kid, at least at the start. The night was slow, and he was company. Then he just turned."

I raised my hamburger. "What do you mean by 'he just turned'?"

"Just that. He turned around one hundred and eighty degrees. He was happy. Then he turned sour. He began to hate this and hate that. There was nothing good for him in all of Clermont County. Heck, Sam, what's a young single guy got here in Greens Point?"

Tucker brushed his hand back over his long salt-and-pepper flattop.

I passed the answer for a salty fry.

"He started talking mean, negative," Tucker continued. "He was talking about death. He kept mumbling things about Holy Hill, nonsense like that. He was saying, 'We'll all wind up on Holy Hill, preacher man and drunk alike.'"

"He got you there, didn't he?"

"Don't you start up. Most young men give up now and then. They all grow out of it. Tommy, he was just down on himself. That's all."

I kept looking at my empty plate. Tucker slapped on some more fries. I didn't want him to catch on to my investigation.

"Did he say anything else about Holy Hill?"

"He was just rambling."

"Do you recall anything in particular?"

"He rattled on about big headstones."

"He did, did he? What did he say?"

"Let me see." Tucker scratched his whiskers. "He said, 'No sense bragging from a headstone.'"

"How about that Tommy? He's come to be a real-life, drunken philosopher, hasn't he?"

"That's just nonsense."

"I'm not too sure about that. Did he say anything else about those big headstones?"

"Nothing important."

"Why do you say that? What else did he say?"

"Believe me, he was talking drunk."

"Come on, now. What'd he say?"

"What's this got to do with a broken picture window?"

"Memory, intent, mental state. Heck, everybody knows you have to be in your right mind to be responsible for committing a crime."

"Sure, I know that."

"Okay. Now, what did he say?"

"All right, Mr. Sheriff. He said, 'I got a mind to piss open every one of those graves.'"

"You don't say?"

"I don't. Tommy said so."

I finished the salty fries and pushed away the empty plate. "That sounds spiteful, doesn't it?"

"No. You know Tommy. That's just drunk talk."

"I suppose you're right."

Tucker took away the empty plate. I started reflecting. I was wondering if that so-called drunk talk was just a simple coincidence with the Albrecht grave. Tommy, I figured, wouldn't have dug up a grave. The demon booze, though, might have.

Regardless of my ruminations, Tommy was long gone for the night. I'd have to approach him in that melancholy morning hangover of his. After he tied one on, he would grow really despondent on the following morning. He would try jacking up his spirits with joke after joke. His grasps at humor made me all the more certain that he was feeling low. The short pops of humor would not buoy him up. They would melt away, leaving him low. If there was some truth to tell, Tommy would tell it during his black state, if he was ever going to tell it.

"Thanks for dinner."

"Thanks for getting Tommy out of here."

I stood up. "I suppose you'll drop the charges if he pays you for the window, won't you?"

"I suppose so. But give it to him good, won't you? Busted windows ain't good for business. You know what I mean?"

I looked around the empty bar.

"Busted windows could only help your business. You know what I mean?"

"Go on. Get out of here. I give you a free dinner, and you tell me such things. Honest, Sam. In the next election, I just might vote against you."

"Sure. And if you're lucky, for once, I won't be running unopposed."

"You keep talking cocky. Maybe I'll sell this joint and run against you."

"Please, do. The town could use a landslide, and the *Bugler* could use the story."

He shooed me out with a flap of his hand. I was ready to leave. The heartburn was starting early.

On the following morning, when I entered the office, Tommy was still sleeping off his hangover. I made a pot of coffee and tossed in an extra spoonful of coffee grinds. After I finished the *Bugler*, he was rustling, so I opened up his cell.

"Tommy?"

He grunted.

"How about a cup of coffee?"

He grunted again, so I fetched him a mug of hot black coffee. I rinsed the empty mug free of the bouillon salt and filled it with coffee. "How's your head?"

"It's still on, ain't it?"

I chuckled and shook my head. He always tossed out that line on the following morning.

"Here."

He rolled over and grabbed the mug. He looked crushed. His dark brown hair was scattered all over his head. He had dark circles under his eyes that matched his hair color. The time had come for truth—or as close to the truth as I was going to get. "Tommy, what were you up to last night?"

"Oh, Sheriff."

"Don't start oh-sheriffing me. I have my duty. You know you busted out Tucker's window."

"I'll pay."

"I know you'll pay. You better pay too. You're lucky Tucker's an all-right guy."

"I know."

"Did you ever think what would happen if Tucker closed the bar on you?"

That line brought a grin on Tommy's face. "Yeah. He'd put himself out of business."

I turned my face to hide my grin. That Tommy was a clever young fellow and likable, too, when sober. "That's beside the point. What got you so drunk?"

"Things."

"You need a woman."

He grinned again. I was ready for his reply.

"I know, Sheriff. You know one?"

"Where were you before Tucker's? I have to write my report."

"I wish I could help you write your report. But the fact of the matter is that I hardly recall being in Tucker's place."

"Your mind isn't that shot."

"I wish it wasn't. I got less than half my brain left to get me through the rest of my life."

"If you keep this up, you won't make it."

"I'm afraid that's true. I'm going to hate closing down Tucker. He's an all-right guy."

Toward the end of our conversation, Tommy joked less and less. The jokes were having less and less effect upon his mood. The melancholy began to set in. He slipped through his black state and hit rock bottom.

Tommy was basically good. He had climbed through life on the back of his jokes. I wasn't going to get anywhere with him. I left him alone in his cell. I called the garage and told Miller that he wasn't going to be working that day. Miller knew. The whole town knew Tommy had a drinking problem. The whole town knew, though, he was the only good mechanic in town and one of the best in the county. He serviced the county cars regularly. I never had a problem with the cars.

Instead of closing, the Albrecht investigation blew wide open. The facts loosely pointed toward Tommy and Norman, so loosely, though, that a tractor could haul a load of hay clear through the gaps. Still, the facts weren't talking to me yet. As I said before, I try not to force facts into speaking. I decided to wait for them to tell me more.

Besides facts, an experienced lawman has his gut instincts. I didn't feel Tommy or Norman had anything to do with digging up the Albrecht grave. Things didn't make sense. I hadn't forgotten the demon booze. At the early stage of the investigation, of all known possibilities, booze had the inside track.

✵ ✵ ✵

During those spring floods, no matter how many sandbags surround Cairo, the Ohio and Mississippi Rivers reclaim a part of the city's limits. Human thought and muscle can't prevent the overflowing rivers, swollen with fresh spring rains. That spring, just like those mighty rivers and Cairo, Greens Point was swamped with grave poaching.

For the next few days, I was successful in my endeavors to ignore the problem at Holy Hill, in the hope of the problem passing away quietly or solving itself. I might say I was growing a little cocky. But as commonly said, humility is the greatest virtue. About a week after Haney's call, Haney called again.

"Sam," Haney began. "I got two more graves dug up on me. I got Norman here in my office." During this second call, Haney displayed absolutely no emotion. He was crushed.

Three graves sort of prodded me off of my rule of thumb to let problems work themselves out. Jessie Daniels from the *Bugler* soon caught scent of the grave poaching and began chasing me with phone calls. She told me she had to answer to the people, whatever that meant. I knew it meant that, at least, I would have to tell my deputies.

Jessie made matters worse. She was a hard-driving woman. The paper was her life. She stuck her nose into everybody's business for a story or a scoop, as she called it.

She focused her attention on her writing, not her looks. She wore her dull light-brown hair shoulder length in that straight and stringy fashion of the younger women in Springfield. She had a thin, rather long nose that began to curl down at the tip. The eyelashes over her beady eyes were never coated with mascara.

I don't have anything against women wearing pants, because women on the farm have been wearing pants for years. But, I swear, I never saw Jessie at a social function or in church on Sundays, when she did show up, wearing a dress.

She had attended Southern Illinois University at Carbondale and brought back to Greens Point that self-righteous determination gleaming from college kids, especially journalism students. I wish she had stayed in that college town or taken that attitude to some big city. Greens Point didn't need her prodding the town in step with the change in times.

When she did get through to me, I told her I'd get back to her later in the day or, at the latest, on the following morning. For the rest of the week, I climbed down the back stairs of the sheriff's office to avoid people out front. I had things on my mind, plus I was conducting my investigation in secret, so as not to tip off the culprits. I managed to slip into the squad car I parked in back of the office and drive down Main Street without talking to a soul.

When I knocked on Haney's office door, I got no response. When I walked into his office, he was more or less in a stupor. He sat in his old torn chair. He answered only once: "Norman is out back. He'll be back in a moment."

I should say Haney had only one answer, because he told me that every time I tried to talk to him.

Norman entered the office about five minutes after my arrival. He was a real trouper. Haney pointed his finger—or his whole hand, I should say—at him. Still, and fortunately for me, he was the person in Greens Point who stood the strongest. I'm not saying he wasn't nervous. Lord knows, he was. Regardless, he helped me. He knew I needed help, and he felt good to be needed.

At times like these, I felt slight misgivings about being a lawman. I couldn't ignore Norman's willingness to help me. His willingness could have been a clue. All sorts of reasons could have explained his willingness: his job as a gravedigger, his ability or strength to assist me, his stupidity to refuse or flee, or his darn good nature. At that moment in the investigation, I still thought the explanation rested in the latter, the most basic being his joy in being needed by someone.

The part of being a lawman I disliked the most was not trusting a soul. My official duty forced me to think ways that were sometimes distasteful. Betsy had a different slant on the problem. In her eyes, every person was good, God's child. Every person deserved the benefit of the doubt. On my side of the law, though, the sheriff was out to arrest on probable cause, and the prosecutor was out to convict beyond a reasonable doubt. Betsy could always find a reasonable doubt. With luck and my position in the county, however, she never served on a jury.

"Thanks for coming out," I said.

He gave me an uneasy smile and shrugged.

"Do you know where to go?" I asked.

"Mr. Haney said the south and east rises," he answered.

"Are you ready?"

"The shovels and mallet are outside."

At this stage of the investigation, I had big doubts about considering him as a suspect. I believed more than one person had to be committing such crimes. From the same modus operandi, I believed the same culprits committed the crimes. He was the only soul on my side. Still, being a lawman, I had to keep an open, suspicious mind.

As we walked through Holy Hill, I felt better and easier than I'd felt during my first walk with Haney. Holy Hill was blooming after the annual downpour washed off winter. Most of the dead brown leaves had been rinsed off the boughs. Crisp green leaves were unfolding on the branches. Norman fit out there, along the rolling slopes. I walked with a friend to the trees and bushes rather than with an invader into a propped-up setting for a business of burial. The magnolia flowers, cupped upward and outward, were beginning to blossom. The magnolias welcomed him.

The graves brought my wondering thoughts back down to earth. Benjamin Wilson rested beneath the tallest headstone on the east rise. Jerome Taylor rested beneath the second tallest headstone on the south rise. Both of the headstones were huge and ornamental. The east rise was set away from the winding road, like the south rise. Both the Wilson and Taylor graves, like the Albrecht grave, were beyond eyesight and earshot of the office.

Although the Wilson and Taylor graves were dug up like the Albrecht grave, there were notable differences in the two just discovered. The lids of the coffins were completely broken off the trunks. The decomposed suits were twisted and torn. To me, the grave poachers seemed to have violated the graves with greater anger.

Norman was as quiet and obedient as a first-grader sentenced to a corner of the classroom for talking. He did what I told him without seeing what I was doing, or so I thought.

As I stood beside the dug-up Wilson grave, I felt the cold spring rain rise up out of the spongy earth into the souls of my boots. A shiver shot down my spine.

There are times when religion really hits home. Most of these times have attacked me outside of church. Seeing graves laid bare slit a haunting gap in my religious bulwark. Honestly, I didn't know which way to look.

That strong, silent Norman stood like a pillar. I saw a simple man doing a job asked of him. After the coffins were pounded shut and the graves filled, we walked back to the office.

"I wish you hadn't seen all of this," I said.

"Seein' is believin'," he replied.

"Right now, I wish I knew what I believed."

"It ain't hard. We seen evil. That's the devil's work. That's what it is. There ain't no good in diggin' up a man's grave."

"That may be true. But I have to catch a thief."

"He's no thief. Even thieves don't steal from the dead."

"Still, I've got to investigate these acts under the laws of the State of Illinois."

"You can call it what you want. But it's plain evil."

Lawmen can get lost among the laws. Norman saw through the courts, legislature, and laws. I was dealing with the lowest grade of human being possible. Big-city murder and rape were one thing, but grave poaching was another. The vile nature of the grave poaching made my task all the worst. I feared calling the Sangamon County sheriff in Springfield or the Cook County sheriff in Chicago for help with these crimes. The last thing Clermont County needed was such bad publicity. Grave poaching three graves in Clermont County was like Gacy's killing thirty-three boys and young men in Cook County.

I was starting to think I'd better call up north for some help. I didn't particularly feel like I needed any help solving the crimes, but I did want some advice on attempting to control the flood of alarm that the press would send throughout the county, state, and even the country.

I was growing concerned that grave poaching might damage the reputation of the county. I knew mass murders sprouted up around the country, mostly though, in or around big cities. There were Manson's murders around Los Angeles and Speck's murders in Chicago. Big cities are known for such atrocities. But grave robbery just doesn't occur anywhere and especially not in a small southern town. I was beginning to feel the mighty Mississippi and Ohio rising up on me without the time or manpower for the sandbagging.

I collected my observations on my notepad so as to save time and duplication of Haney's records. I made a special review of the headstones. I had taken photographs of the headstones, the locations of the graves, and the condition of the corpses before Norman and I laid them again to rest. Before leaving Holy Hill, I left word with Haney for the records, even though I figured I had collected as much information from the headstones as he could copy. I had to hit all sources in my investigation.

Based upon my observations at the grave sites, review of documents, and discussions with some of the oldest citizens in Greens Point, I came up with profiles of Benjamin Wilson and Jerome Taylor. I skipped Wally. He couldn't have firsthand knowledge, and I didn't have time for jokes. Jerome Taylor was laid to rest just before the turn of the twentieth century. The Taylor headstone was the second tallest headstone on the south rise. Jerome Taylor had owned the biggest barge operation on the Ohio along the southeastern border of Illinois.

Benjamin Wilson's grave was marked by the tallest headstone on the east rise. Later, I learned, and rumor so had it, that Benjamin Wilson bought out the entire east rise for his family and friends. Good will was one reason, but dominance was the main reason. By personally plotting out the entire east rise, Benjamin Wilson was guaranteed the tallest headstone. That was some foresight back then. Benjamin Wilson's acreage cuffed the entire northeastern rim of Greens Point and nearly the remainder of that section of Clermont County. Once again, the graves beneath the tallest headstones were invaded, and correspondingly, the old money of Greens Point was raided.

Chapter 5

To this day, I still don't know who Haney told. Regardless, Jeb's phone messages from Jessie indicated she was tracking the graves. In an attempt to head off a possible stampede, I called her. In less than five minutes, she was sitting across my desk with her pen and pad in hand.

"Do you have any suspects for the grave robberies?"

"Now, Miss Daniels—"

"Ms. Daniels."

"Ms. Daniels, slow down a second here. I haven't even said the word 'robberies.'"

"So you don't think the graves were robbed?"

"I haven't had a chance to begin to tell you anything yet."

Jessie Daniels would interview a dying man if she smelled a story from him.

"Just ask your questions one at a time and give me time in between them to answer."

"Don't you think there's a connection between the Albrecht, Taylor, and Wilson graves?"

"From the size of the headstones and my background check, I'd say all three men were well off."

"Don't those facts suggest grave robbery?"

"Yes, they might suggest it."

Actually, the facts were now shouting grave poaching at me.

"Sheriff, you sealed and covered the coffins before I was able to see the bodies. Did the clothes or bodies appear to be tampered with?"

"That's a good question."

"If that's a compliment, I thank you, but I didn't come here for compliments. I came here for facts. I have to tap all sources in my investigation."

Admittedly, although I was not particularly fond of her, I never claimed she was stupid or a bad reporter. I was hoping I could have slid through her interview without being confronted with that question.

"My duties and the pending investigation bar me from answering that question."

"As a reporter for the people of this community, I feel I have a right to know all the facts."

I was ready for her we-the-people speech. I gave her mine back. "I'm sorry you feel that way. I, however, was elected the sheriff by the people of Clermont County. If I missed your name on the ballot, please forgive me. I have a duty to the people to enforce the laws of this state to the best of my abilities. So, at this stage of the investigation, I repeat my duties and the pending investigation bar me from discussing the condition of the corpses or clothes."

"I don't have time to fight with a lawman. May I have a copy of your report?"

"I'm not finished yet. I wouldn't want to give you and the people a partial picture of the investigation."

"Fine, Sheriff. I see I'm getting nowhere with you. Thanks for your time."

She slapped her notepad shut and stormed out the front door—the door I could use again. If I had known the interview was going to be so harmless, I would have talked to her on day one.

After she called on me about the graves and I spent a good deal of time sizing up the situation, I decided to call a meeting of my five deputies in the office for three o'clock. Old Jeb Stuart had been a deputy sheriff even before my terms as the sheriff. His age and rheumatism, especially during the spring and fall rains, slowed him down considerably. I assigned him to the office. He cleaned the jail cells in the back room, took out the garbage, and answered the telephone. He was good at those duties, when his rheumatism wasn't acting up.

Hank Turner was a hard-charging lawman, sometimes too hard. Upon somebody's advice, I forget whose, I took him on right after I was sworn in my first term. At that time, I figured hard charging was better than no charging. He looked like a lawman. He was broad shouldered and lean waisted with smooth, oiled down jet-black hair. Since then, I've grown fonder of his wife and children than him. Even Hank, though, would have trouble messing up petty offenses—so I thought.

Outside of town, I assigned Rusty Jenkins to basically cover north of town, especially Feegan's Bluff, the second city behind Greens Point in Clermont County. Rusty lived on the outskirts of Feegan's Bluff. Rusty and Hank would come to butt heads over my spot when I stepped down. Rusty had the instincts, but Hank had the drive.

Billy Ray Spoons was something else. His grandfather was Senator Charles Spoons, who represented our part of southeastern Illinois for years. I was kind of pressed to take on young Billy Ray. So, as not to bother the town and me, I assigned him to traffic detail along all the country roads outside of Greens Point and the other towns.

In addition to Jeb, Hank, Rusty, and Billy Ray, I had a deputy sheriff assigned to the county courthouse as a more-or-less bailiff. John Day, a big, burly fellow with a bum foot, led the defendants in and out of the courtroom holding cell, when there were defendants. He mostly ran simple errands for Judge Flynn.

At two forty-five, Hank threw open the office door. Jeb was already resting in a corner chair next to John. Hank poured himself a cup of coffee and didn't sit. Hank seemed steamed up. I figured he had heard about the grave poaching before the meeting. He was an embarrassed lawman. It would take some doing to calm him down to listen. Rusty strolled in a couple minutes before three.

Hank stepped up to my desk. "Let's start the meeting," he said.

"Let's wait for Billy Ray," I said.

Hank rolled away from my desk, like a bull turning around to gore. "I'm not going to wait a minute for Billy."

"We'll wait a bit for Billy Ray."

The five of us waited until ten after three. Then the office door swung open, and Billy Ray walked into the office.

"Sorry I'm late. I was far out on a country road."

Billy Ray was always far out on a country road. His life had been spent far out on one long winding road.

"Pull up a chair," I told them all.

None of them did. Jeb and John stayed in the corner. Rusty leaned against a wall, and Hank kept pacing. Billy Ray stood off in a corner.

"I guess you all know the reason for the meeting."

Jeb, John, and Billy Ray were looking at me. Rusty was thinking about something he had probably done earlier in the day. Hank was gazing off above us.

"In all of my terms, I've never faced such a grave situation."

Hank shot a look at me for my choice of words.

"If you haven't heard the whole story yet, then I'll fill you in. Three graves have been dug up at Holy Hill: Henry Albrecht, Benjamin Wilson, and Jerome Taylor. The headstones were the biggest in the cemetery. The corpses were, well, what can I say, looted. Pockets were turned inside out, and rotten suits were ripped. Possibly important, I didn't see a belt or shoes in the Albrecht grave."

Nobody yet reacted to me. I thought they might be still angry at me for withholding the information. I knew Hank was.

"The condition of the corpses leads me to believe the culprits were grave poachers. They dug in the pockets for watches and searched for any jewelry, silver, or gold they could find."

Hank couldn't hold back any longer. "Do you have any physical evidence of 'grave poaching,' as you call it?"

"What kind are you asking about?" I asked.

"Did you dust for fingerprints?"

"No. Then again, I don't believe we still have that dusting kit."

"Did you recover any boot prints?"

"No."

"Then, what evidence, hard, scientific evidence, do you have for your 'grave poaching'?"

"Nothing positive."

"What's that mean?" Hank asked.

"In the absence of an earthquake tossing up the graves from beneath the three biggest headstones in Holy Hill, I kind of just figured somebody dug up the graves. I don't know the scientific name for it, Hank, but I call it common sense. What's more, common sense tells me that the digger wasn't that lonely to see his long-lost relatives."

"You can't get too far on common sense."

"I can start, can't I? Besides, in case you don't recall so well, when the graves were busted open, you were off fishing in the Shawnee National Forest with the county prosecutor."

Old Jeb, he was chuckling away. Jeb's stomach was rolling up and down from his brass belt buckle to his rib cage and back. Off in the corner,

Billy Ray wore a bitter smile on his face. He was almost thin enough to hide behind the wooden coat-tree his hand was hanging on. Hank was being nothing but ornery. He wouldn't look me straight in the eye the whole time I spoke. In his evasion, he was trying to show he was above all of us.

"So, Sam, what's next?" Jeb asked to wedge a truce between Hank and me.

"That's the reason I called this meeting. Jeb, you handle the phone calls like you always do. Basically, take messages, get names and numbers, but don't give out any information."

"Gotcha." Jeb gave me a wink.

"Billy Ray, you keep your eyes open for drifters passing through the county who don't look right. Pull them over on anything that might stick and then open your eyes when you question them in their vehicles."

"Like busted tail lights?"

"Ease up a bit on those tail lights, Billy Ray. The judge is starting to ask questions."

Hank kept staring straight ahead.

"Hank, you just hang tight until we get some leads."

"Sam, leads won't walk down the street and knock on the office door."

"Maybe not. But if we keep low, we won't scare off any suspects."

"John, keep your ears open in the lockup."

John nodded back to me. There wasn't much more he could do in an empty lockup with that bum foot of his.

"Rusty, I may need you down here. I'll keep you posted."

"Whatever you say."

For the rest of the meeting, I related most of everything I saw at Holy Hill. Old, chubby Jeb kept a rattled grin on his face. Billy Ray stood silently and a bit stiff. Hank stared off, casting his arrogant importance.

My line about the fishing trip wounded Hank. I'm sure he and Bob Hunt were plotting politics while they were off fishing. But as luck and timing happened to meet, the grave robberies broke open with neither of them in town. Plainly speaking, they got caught with their pants down. Rusty, in his quiet way, was stepping more closely behind me as my successor. In turn, Hank was trying to draw a support base with Bob Hunt.

I closed the meeting with all promising to keep a tight lip, especially to Jessie Daniels. Only I had the authority through my position to talk to the press. Jeb didn't care to talk. He had nothing to gain. Billy Ray hadn't the guts or smarts to talk, in fear of making a mistake. Hank might talk to boost his career. But if I kept the important information to myself, he'd have nothing to say. Besides, if Hank leaked a story, I'd know it was him from all of his personal references in the story.

✳ ✳ ✳

All folks who think Illinois is one big suburb of Chicago are really fooled. The southern third of the state is covered with rolling hills, forests, lakes, and streams, offering fine hunting and fishing. From the west, the Ozark Mountains come rolling to Illinois and are laid to rest down here. The tip of our state drops south past the middle of Kentucky.

The day following our meeting was warm and sunny, so I decided to spend the afternoon investigating outdoors. Towns throughout Southern Illinois are picture postcards: town squares, church steeples, hardware stores with bags of seed and fertilizer out front, and diners. I took advantage of the weather to investigate four more cemeteries. St. Peter's Cemetery was on the outskirts of Greens Point. A small group of Catholic farmers and tradesmen lived out in that part of the county. St. Peter's Church stood along the road in front of the cemetery. The church was a small white wooden-framed building. The little red brick house next to the church was the rectory. Father Kiel was the pastor and only priest for miles around.

When I pulled the squad car into the drive by the rectory, I saw him straighten up behind the rectory in a tiny garden. He gave me a wave, and I walked over to him.

"I always plant the marigolds first. They keep the bugs away."

He swept a fly off his forehead.

Although I had known that trick for years, I didn't let on. "I'll give Betsy the tip."

He clapped the dirt from his hands. He was a slim Irishman with thin dark hair. His face was red, probably from the exertion and not the sun. He always tried to act so robustly. But, despite the dirt on his hands, his garden would come up again thin and parched.

"What brings you out this way, Sheriff?"

"I suppose I'll just ask you straight off. Have you had any problems out back in the cemetery?"

He smiled.

"No. I suspected as much. You see, I read the *Bugler*. I checked over the cemetery just today."

"Do you mind if I check it out?"

"Not at all."

"Thanks, Father."

"I'll save you some tomatoes."

I chuckled at the earnest little priest.

St. Peter's Cemetery was small and plain. Decades ago, the Catholic Church came down on cemetery statuary. The Church edict and lack of money among the parishioners resulted in small headstones laid in the earth above the head of the grave. St. Peter's was set out in farmland on the outer rim of choice land. Consequently, the cemetery was flat. Shade trees had been planted but had grown poorly. My walk was brief. He wasn't mistaken. I saw nothing peculiar in the cemetery.

There was a potter's field cut out plunk down in the center of the county within a lightly forested area. Masonry half-columns connected by metal pickets lined the country road. There was no office or church for this field grown wild. In my estimation, there hadn't been a burial in the field since maybe the Second or even the First World War. The children about town called the field Bachelor's Row. Teenagers would drive out to the field in the black of night for a scare every Halloween. When I was young, I had gone out for a scare.

Although my vision from the squad car wasn't the best, I didn't see anything worth investigating close up on foot. I stayed in the county car and drove quickly through the field.

Galesboro is a sleepy little town that sits northwest of Greens Point about thirty miles. That town had sprouted up like a prairie flower. I can't think of a reason for the birth of that town. Galesboro has no access to water, a railroad, or a state highway. Yet Galesboro ranked third behind Feegan's Bluff and Greens Point in population in Clermont County.

Galesboro has a main street a block long, lined with shops. Fifteen minutes from that main street is Golden Gate Cemetery. Inside the front gate off to the right, the office and garage sat. The office appeared bigger and newer than Haney's. I parked the county car and walked into the office.

"Good day, sir, or should I say, Sheriff?"

A short man, dressed sporty, stood up from behind a huge desk. He had thin, wiry black hair with a few sprouts of gray. His face glowed with that naturally distilled red flush.

I extended my hand. "Sheriff Sam Carter, Clermont County."

We shook hands.

"Sure, Sheriff Sam Carter. I see your name every election year. I'm Tom Bussie. What brings you out this way? You aren't looking for more open graves? Aren't three enough?"

He belted out a laugh that forced his shoulders to flap up and down so hard that they'd have fallen right off if they weren't somehow attached.

"You're right, Tom. How've things been here at Golden Gate?"

"Heavenly."

He belted out two muffled snorts of laughter through his nostrils. "I have no problems. If I did, I would have called you."

"When's the last time you were out around the cemetery?"

"Why, just the other day."

I detected that loose, easy overconfidence that meant he was lying through those well-picked white teeth of his.

"Do you mind if I take a look?"

"Absolutely not. I'll come along if you want me."

I extended my hand to the front door.

His eyebrows dropped a bit on my acceptance. The maroon-and-silver inner lining flashed before my eyes as he slipped into his black suit coat.

He talked mostly to fill the silence. He bragged on and on about Golden Gate. After the first minute of our cruise, I was beginning to suspect he was dealing me a sales pitch for a plot.

I'll give him credit. Golden Gate was well kept, bushes trimmed and lawn mowed. Shade trees spotted the fairly flat cemetery. With his assistance, I managed to complete an investigation of another cemetery without getting out of the car. We saw nothing unusual, and I had a lot of ground to cover. We parted with another one of Tom's belts of laughter.

Although I was starting to wear down from the investigation, I had planned to make one more stop before dinner. Feegan's Bluff was a drive for about an hour southeast of Galesboro. Feegan's Bluff was the second jewel in the Illinois crown on the Ohio River. Dating back to before the Civil War, Greens Point and Feegan's Bluff had competed for the riverboat traffic on the Ohio. Green's Point had won that battle, but Feegan's Bluff at present seemed to have won the war. Because Feegan's Bluff didn't grow as large, the town also didn't have to sink as low with the passage of time.

As a matter of fact, Feegan's Bluff was beginning to draw vacation and tour money into the town coffers. Within my last term, St. Louis and Cincinnati tourists had begun paying money to float down the Mississippi and Ohio Rivers on renovated steamboats. Trips lasted from a day to a long weekend or even to a week or more. The steamboats had stopovers every so many miles. Feegan's Bluff had a scheduled stopover for one of the main outfits. The stopovers helped the restaurants and shops. Feegan's Bluff had added a restaurant, a gift shop, and an antique shop. The town unloaded a lot of its old furniture at a good price for used furniture.

I supposed Greens Point could have used the money, but I wasn't too sure the town could have withstood the tourists. Tourists prey on commercialization. I just don't know if I would have liked tourists watching me, the sheriff, walk up and down Main Street. I'm sure bold city dwellers would have stopped me to joke about the absence of murder, rape, and violent crimes in Greens Point. And of course, I would have been polite and responded that Greens Point didn't have all of the luxuries associated with big cities. We could get by on our own.

I arrived in Feegan's Bluff in good time before supper. I remembered that the big cemetery was fifty yards west of the town's Baptist church, which was the last building on the west end of the main street. Members of the congregation said the cemetery was open to the public, evidenced by the fifty-yard separation from the church, but the town and I knew better. The cemetery was a Baptist cemetery, but the segregation didn't mean much to a town predominantly Baptist.

The cemetery was noticeably bigger than Haney's. Magnolias broke up the landscape. I walked into the office and waited thirty seconds after the bell on the door jangled. A middle-aged man with greasy blond hair and thick eyeglasses stepped into the room. "I'm sorry. Mr. Jacobs is ill today." Seeing my tan uniform and manner, the man continued, "How may I help you?"

"I'm Sheriff Sam Carter, Clermont County sheriff."

"I'm Perry Smith. I'm standing in for Mr. Jacobs."

"I've stopped in on business."

"I bet you're here on the grave robberies. I read Jesse Daniels's article."

"Yes, Jessie Daniels. She's a good reporter, isn't she?"

"She's the best we have down here."

From the looks of him, I figured he would have said as much.

"I'm the English teacher at the high school."

"I noticed you spoke real fine."

Mr. Smith was almost six feet tall and terribly thin. He wore eyeglasses with thick black frames and a neat part down the right side of his thick greasy hair. His complexion looked oily, red, and sore. "I'm only a substitute.

I don't know too much, especially about the graves. I primarily answer the telephone and continue matters a day or so until Mr. Jacobs is back."

"You wouldn't mind if I take a drive around, would you?"

"No, I can't see why not."

I took that drive. The cemetery was a good deal bigger than Holy Hill. Since I had been driving all day, I decided to stretch my legs. I pulled to the side of a winding road and walked behind a row of lilac bushes bearing a trace of their sweet scent.

Behind the lilacs, I saw nothing but tranquility. I leaned up against the thick, tough bark of an old oak tree and gazed out over the quiet cemetery. Over the half hour behind the lilacs, I spotted two blue jays by a pine tree. I almost always spot blue jays by pines or evergreens. I also saw a male cardinal, sharp red, in flight toward another oak. The male blue jay's radar-sounding call seemed to echo about the tree trunks in the empty cemetery. On a much weaker scale, the cardinal's faint beeping seemed to fall to the ground twenty yards off the bough the bird had found.

Southern Illinois is plentiful with brightly painted birds. Although the cardinal is the state bird, my favorite has always been the blue jay. Against the soft, green southern pines, the sharp blues of the bird stand out. The head crest rolls back from its face and beak, and its chest and throat are pushed upward and outward as the call radiates out into the fields.

I climbed back into the squad car to finish my inspection. After ten minutes, I headed for home. I pulled up in the drive late for dinner. I knew Betsy would understand. She would support me in every little way she could. She would warn me not to act without firm belief. She was the eternal heart for all souls forgotten or downtrodden. Even if we didn't agree on points in my investigation, I had to side with her beliefs at home.

When I entered our home, I smelled chicken and gravy warming in the oven. She was bathing while listening to the radio. I called out to her when I entered, and she called to me to take the chicken out of the oven. I pulled the chicken out of the oven and ate dinner alone in the kitchen.

About the time I finished my dinner, she walked into the kitchen in her quilted robe, with her hair up in a towel. "Tough day, honey?" she asked me.

"You betcha."

"There've been calls most of the day."

"I'm sorry, dear. You know I don't have control over those calls."

"I know. I won't worry you about those calls. You have your work cut out for you. You can do anything, if you approach it one step at a time."

We talked for maybe an hour in general about the graves, the investigation, and Jessie Daniels's article in the *Bugler*. From reading the article, she seemed as well informed as me. She was fond of Tommy and Norman. According to her, neither could have committed those acts. She believed nobody in Greens Point could have dug up a grave, let alone three. Of course, she admitted she was not the sheriff. Nevertheless, she believed suspecting anybody in town, especially Tommy or Norman, didn't make sense.

"Common sense is the rudder in life," she said. "If you lose the rudder, you lose the way."

According to Betsy, life makes sense if you don't overthink it. The problem is we may not know it. She can coin life into simple little phrases and live by them too.

Chapter 6

I CAN'T recall any event that upset Greens Point more than the grave poaching. Jesse Daniels set the town buzzing with her article in the *Bugler* on the day following my meeting with her. With the exception of some additional history on Albrecht, Taylor, and Wilson, her article provided no further information than that uncovered in my investigation.

The town was a bit uneasy. The laid-back lives of our townsfolk had been rustled. Some wrong was looming off in the distance, like a storm cloud cuffing the Ohio River Valley. Despite the sunny spring days with the warm breezes whipping up from the river valley, shadows seemed to collect up and down Main Street on people's faces.

The nature of the crime made my job all the more difficult. There was little I could do, so I did little. There was no hard charging to do. A straight, simple direct attack was impossible.

I had done all I could do. I inspected all the graves. I collected what little records Haney could produce. After the Taylor and Wilson graves were discovered, I again interviewed Norman and Tommy. Norman was in his shed, reading, playing the harmonica, or sleeping. Even though he had no alibi witnesses, I believed him. Besides, he had no family or friends to provide an alibi. What's more, he was just too simple for such a bizarre crime.

Tommy had come off his binge, or perhaps he was on the downside of his binge. He drank moderately to come off slowly. After work in the garage, he had been stopping in at Tucker's for a few beers. Tucker doesn't hold a grudge, so long as Tommy's got change in his pocket. Besides, beer is low octane for Tommy. Tucker steered him away from the sour mash. Whereas the booze may have dug up the graves, Tommy hadn't. With Tommy mostly off the heavy sauce, I became more certain he had nothing to do with the graves.

In Greens Point, if anybody wants to know what's happened lately, that person should first go to the drugstore. Ben Olson knows who's been taking what for what. He's kind of quiet sometimes, but Ethel, his cashier, sure isn't. She loves to tell anybody why anybody has been in the store. She acts like she has some secret power nobody else has. If a man can't find something out at Olson's Drugstore, then he should try the barber shop and talk to Herman, who still gives a good shave. If he doesn't need a haircut, then he and his wife need only congregate on the church stoop after Sunday service.

I found assurance in Herman's opinions. I'd wager a couple bucks that Greens Point is the only county seat in Illinois with a barber, not a hair stylist, for men. We still use Herman's as a hitching post to gather and talk. Plain talk on a barber's chair is soothing. Almost every man in Greens Point has sat in his chair, except for a few of the farmers who lived far out on the rim of the county, whose wives cut their hair.

His position offered him a good opportunity to be the ears of Greens Point. Besides listening, he loved to talk. Talking helped him pass the time of day. He was short, with barely perceptible gray hairs sprouting out around his ears. He wore eyeglasses, probably from the daily strain on his eyes. The lenses made his eyes look a little big. He had an easy manner and soft voice. He talked almost in a whisper. Both his manner and voice supported a gentle conversation while he clipped away. Betsy thought he clipped too much, which made my ears look big, but I like a close, cool cut.

He advised me that most men figured the culprits were from out of town. He said most believed the culprits were drifters with no roots anywhere in the county.

In his opinion, and he spoke then even more quietly, he believed ex-cons did the digging. When pushed, he had no reasons for his belief. But he believed the worse was over and all would pass. He figured the culprits made what little score they could and had long gone. Any more agitating the community would only lead to their capture. He figured any men smart enough to dig up three graves were smart enough to let well enough alone.

I questioned his last line of logic on the culprits' intelligence, and he told me to just wait and see. At the end of my haircut, he thought the town should be grateful that the convicts didn't turn on the town and rob us at gunpoint. I said I wasn't too sure if grave poaching was anything the town should be grateful for. He wasn't so sure then either, and we left it at that. I thanked him for the haircut and opinions.

I was hoping his opinions were correct. In a month, the grave poaching would begin to pass out of the minds of the townsfolk. By letting the problem alone and not aggravating it, all might settle right. Of course, I didn't tell him my thoughts. I didn't want the public to start thinking I wasn't concerned. Laying off or, I should say, laying back is my way of taking care of business.

Even when I wasn't in the midst of my investigation, those two drifters under the bridge kept popping up in my mind. But I couldn't just go searching for them. I had no probable cause to arrest them, and I didn't even know what crimes had been committed.

✳ ✳ ✳

Although there wasn't much the town or I could do, Reverend Betts must have felt he could do something. Thinking back, that Sunday sermon was his most forceful ever. Instead of the blunt-faced congregation he faced every Sunday, he finally had a congregation pricked by some uncertainty. As a lawman, I grounded my job on certainty in peace, law, and order. Men of the cloth, being lawmen themselves, sort of speaking, thrive on the unknown. Religion is grounded on the unknown. The unknown is the door to belief and compliance with the law of God. In his sermon, he attempted to take his congregation that short but steep step from the unknown to deeper faith. Regardless of the outcome, I have to say that he tried his hardest.

That Sunday was pleasant and sunny. A gentle breeze rustled the ladies' light spring dresses on the stone porch. The heat from the morning sunlight was beginning to release the sweet smell of the brightly colored flowers around the porch. The church was one of the oldest and prettiest buildings in town, built solid with stone arched roof and steeple holding the church bell.

A good portion of the congregation sat on the back pews to catch the breeze from the entrance during the reverend's sermon. Fortunately, Betty Butts was back there. She caught most of the breeze. They were back there until air conditioning kicked on for summer. If she passed out up front, the reverend would have to stop his sermon to give all the ushers a hand carrying her out for a breath of fresh air.

Since I was an elected official, I walked up to the front of the church. I sat alone. Betsy was playing the organ.

After songs and preliminaries, the service came to the sermon. The reverend walked slowly to the pulpit. Although short, his stocky frame made him look taller off at a distance than a skinny frame would have. Moreover, his face was wide with bright blue eyes behind wire-rimmed glasses, and his head was round and bony with thin dark hair plastered down around it. This broad appearance also seemed to increase his physical stature.

As he stood behind the pulpit, though, the congregation sitting directly in front of the pulpit could just spot his big head. He held his hands straight out to grip the sides of the pulpit. After reading a passage from the Bible, chapter and verse I forgot, he began his most penetrating sermon.

"In the coming weeks, a trial will begin right here in Greens Point."

He paused, quite consciously, I thought, for effect.

"The faith of each of us in this congregation will be tested. As you all have probably heard, three graves were dug up at Holy Hill. Those acts crack the foundation of the belief of any religious community. Sometime soon, if not already, the line between right and wrong or good and evil will have to be examined."

He charged a bit too hard at the start. That was a gamble. He risked falling flat later in the sermon—a tendency he demonstrated regularly every Sunday.

"I warn you now that the harder that line is examined by each of us alone, the grayer it becomes. If ventured alone, each will be cast adrift reflecting on the value and worth of even the simplest daily tasks, like working, saving, and maybe even attending church service."

The reverend was really good at tossing out scattered statements at his congregation at the start of his sermon and then explaining them all at the end—something like a picture puzzle. "Really good" may be an overstatement. He did it about once a month. The effect is good, if the audience doesn't grow weary of the technique.

As a lawman, I was used to pulling together a jumble of scattered facts. Generally, I correctly guessed the end of the sermon moments after he tossed out his opening lines. I don't know if most of the congregation followed him. Of course, I had an edge over them. I better appreciated his attempt.

"The invasion of those graves pierced the very soul of our community. The invasion violated our divine rite of passage, the sacred burial. Spades smashed our eternal tomb. Our sense of decency was shattered. Our inner sense of security, worth, and redemption was shaken. In response, at least initially, the lay mind is inclined to wonder and even worse doubt.

"A trial is not good or bad in itself," he continued. "A person's response to the trial is the measure of that person. I suppose some persons have always had good fortune in life. I know most of us in the congregation have experienced encounters with disappointment, disheartenment, disillusion, or defeat. The truly good man or woman is not necessarily he or she who has had good fortune throughout life. A person's response to life's misfortunes is the best measure for the truly good. A person is only as good as his or her response is to victory or, even more so, defeat."

The reverend closed in on his point. "The first step for all of us during troubled times is to steer clear through the ordeal. The truly good person is the person who goes further. The truly good person uses the evil encounter to do good. The worst times are the times to do the greatest good.

"The test is quite simple. Any person sitting in this church can measure the degree to which he or she emerges from the trial to become more Christian in the sense of caring, understanding, and helping."

I glanced over my shoulders around the pews to see how the congregation was taking the sermon. The reverend was doing pretty good so far, but of course he was just warming up. I spotted the white hair and flushed red face of Judge Flynn next to his wife. He appeared to be listening, but I couldn't say if understanding or caring. Bob Hunt, the Clermont County prosecutor, his wife, and children were sitting behind Judge Flynn. Both the judge and Bob were familiar with public speaking, so they were smart enough to understand. Caring might have been their problem. Most of my friends and colleagues were sitting too far back in the church for me to see.

I hoped that the reverend wouldn't cast off on some abstract argument.

"As I briefly touched upon, through a crisis, a Christian can ascend in worth by arising from the crisis as a better Christian. By helping others, a Christian is helping him or herself. The more a person does for another, the better that person becomes. Through dark times, each of us may better see the light. By helping the poor, each of us becomes rich in spirit."

He jumbled up too many ideas at one time. I figured that he would eventually come down from talking abstract generalities and start some down-to-earth preaching.

"Sheriff Carter is faced with a mighty task."

My neck stiffened up on me from that lead by the reverend, although I hoped nobody noticed.

"He has a gruesome task of investigation and one onerous task of prosecution."

Even though he blurred the lines between Bob Hunt and myself, he tried hard and couldn't be faulted for technical blurs. I wondered if Bob was so understanding.

"The sheriff and his wife, Betsy, bless them, have had to live with these horrible acts daily. The sheriff's approach to the problems, however, is a practical one, not a spiritual one."

I gave him my undivided attention.

"The sheriff must investigate with an eye to arrest. The prosecutor then prosecutes, and the judge presides at the trial."

I glanced out of the side of my eyes at Bob Hunt and Judge Flynn. They stiffened up at the neck too.

"Our trial, though, friends in Christ, is not in the county courthouse but outside the courts and law. Our trial is in our daily lives, with each tragedy, setback, and misfortune."

I waited for him to tie up all of his comments and remarks. He was now closing in on us.

"Through each of our personal trials, faith in Christ commands that we stick to the teachings of Jesus. Instead of fretting over our own plight, we should step out to help a neighbor. Instead of remaining frozen in fear or bewilderment, we should reach out to help a neighbor. The problem rests in our own selves, in selfish feelings, thoughts, and desires. The solution is to forget ourself by helping others."

He slowly began to raise his voice. "Shock and horror struck Greens Point. Many of our congregation feel an unfocused fear and possibly distrust. Many may feel as if they should withdraw from their daily acts to seek protection.

"I warn you. Do the opposite of your feelings. Basic Christianity commands true believers to disregard his or her feelings to follow Jesus.

"During this tempest in Greens Point, we should remember and abide by his teachings. When we feel the need to withdraw, we should reach out. When we feel fear, we should gain strength in our faith in God, the Almighty.

"We shall never know all. Only God knows all. As the book of John proclaims, in the beginning, he was with God. He was life, and his life was the light that shines for the world. If we place our trust and our faith in God and we follow Jesus day after day, we shall be rid of doubt, gloom, and fear and led to the good life."

I thought that was the reverend's finest sermon. He grounded his abstractions with concrete examples in the community. Even though his references to me put more pressure on me, my position as an elected official commanded that I bear the weight.

He presented the congregation with a personal way to react to the grave poaching without talking too directly about the graves and scaring the members of the congregation. But the effect of the sermon remained to be seen. Luckily for him, he was taking chances with a congregation and not at a poker table.

The regulars clustered on the church steps after the service in the soft morning sunlight. I waited among them for Betsy to pack her sheet music. I've always found peace stretching my legs on the church steps in the sunlight after Sunday service. On the steps, Reverend Betts was rightfully commended on his sermon. Then each of us went our own way back into Sunday and the approaching week.

✻ ✻ ✻

I can't recall a time when Greens Point was hit harder with bad luck. Muriel Horner died within a week of Reverend Betts's sermon. Haney got the burial.

The weather slipped back cooler with some showers at the beginning of the week, but a change in weather doesn't kill anybody. True, Muriel had caught a cold that slipped into pneumonia. But weather doesn't kill. Her heart stopped ticking. That's all. Doc Adams saw and explained good and simple. Officially, Doc wrote up the cause of her death as a heart attack. Eventually, all of us die of a heart attack, because the heart stops.

I've long gone stopped worrying about death. Everybody's got a ticket. The Maker calls it in. I make death simple to make life simple.

Not to lessen the loss of Muriel, but her death left Norman's situation up in the air. Most of the town knew she had a will, but none of us had ever read it. Her attorney, Bernie Cain of Cain and Polk, certainly had the will.

But Bernie was in Springfield for the week on another case. Ben Polk had been dead for years.

Neither Betsy nor I knew any relatives of Mrs. Horner, at least, close relatives in the county. Gauging from the talk about town, nobody else knew relatives of Mrs. Horner, which put the church in the lead for her estate.

Every soul in Greens Point was speculating on who was to get the Horner acreage. Although the acreage was unkempt, the Horner land took up some of the choicest farmland in the county.

With the rumor circulating all week of the possibility of no natural takers of the farm, Reverend Betts seemed to me to be in an especially good mood. After all, he had been plugging charity from the pulpit since he came into town.

Either nobody in town had the gall to call Mr. Cain in Springfield that week or Mr. Cain didn't have time to return calls. That's the way Bernie was. He was always running around somewhere and usually going nowhere. His desk was generally covered with papers. His hair wasn't combed, and his eyeglasses rested crookedly on his face from bent wire frames, an unbalanced nose, or uneven ears. Regardless, he got the basic jobs done, wills and house closings. Ben Polk, when he was alive, was the opposite, smooth, slow, and well organized. His shoes carried that homemade spit shine. Ben died of a heart attack. He must have kept all his worries inside himself.

Nobody could tell me any news on the Horner property. I felt a duty to discover the future whereabouts of that choice acreage to preserve the smooth transition of property and the peace and order of Greens Point. I thought hard over coffee one morning and came to the only possibility. I called her on the telephone.

"Hello, Ms. Daniels?"

"Of course," she answered.

I've admitted she was a good reporter, but I won't budge an inch on her sour disposition.

"Ms. Daniels, I'm calling in the line of an official investigation."

"Let me save you time, Sheriff. I don't know anything about the Horner will. The will is locked up. If I busted into Cain's office, you'd string me up for burglary and probably try to tie me into the grave robberies," she snapped back.

I let the grave poaching dig slide off my back. "Not all crimes are reported."

"Sorry. When I do get the information before you, I'll report to the readers, not the county."

I had to blunt her freedom-fighter speech. "The county is not that bad of a guy here in Greens Point."

"I don't mean to cut your investigation off short, but I have work to do."

She never gave me a chance. She was forgetting that we were in Greens Point. News in small towns gets around town long before the town paper.

She couldn't beat me to the punch. I had my sources too. After I finally set aside the possibility of a warrant for lack of a crime, lunchtime rolled around. After lunch, I always undertook my official walk up and down Main Street, except on stormy days. I specially calculated my official post-lunch walk to pass by those who knew what was happening in town. Nevertheless, despite my calculations, I only came up with the rumor that the church had the inside track to the property.

✳ ✳ ✳

Bernie Cain came rambling into his office the following Monday morning around ten, as usual. I saw his secretary, Ruth Wright, enter the office five minutes before him. She invited me inside the office. She worked a few hours each morning to type and answer the telephone. She wore lots of facial powder and a tightly curled permanent in her dyed brown hair, the way most of the women her age did in Greens Point. I'm sure she told Bernie about Muriel's death.

As I sat down, Jessie Daniels threw open the front door, marched past me, and stood right in front of Ruth's desk. Jessie turned toward me but didn't have the decency to say hello.

"Sam, how's Betsy?" asked Ruth.

"Good—she couldn't be better. I'll just be a minute."

I rose from my chair and walked into Bernie's office, turning toward Jessie but paying her no greeting.

"Hello," I said to Bernie.

"You're looking good. Grab a chair, while I straighten up here," he replied.

He had a desktop full of telephone messages—most, if not all, of which I'm sure were regarding the Horner estate. He always said that part about straightening up, but he would just glance at the papers on his desk and push them to another spot. I closed his door on Jessie's stare. I pulled up a chair before his big old oak desk.

"How was Springfield?" I asked.

"Too many cars." He flipped through his messages. "Muriel Horner died, eh?" he remarked.

"She died last week," I said.

"I know. Ruth told me."

"Ruth's a good secretary."

"She's a fine lady."

He pushed aside the messages. "From these messages, the town seems to be more interested in her death than her life. Funny how people are, aren't they?" He glanced up over his eyeglasses from the pile of messages.

"I don't try to understand them anymore," I answered. "That's the safe way."

"Well, let me pull her file." With a groan, he pushed himself up from his desk and walked back to a metal file cabinet. He ran his fat, dry thumb over alphabet tab markers, clicking along as he ran. He stopped and pulled out a manila file jacket.

"Let me check my memory for a moment. Let's see now. Yeah, I was right. I don't know who's going to be happier, St. John or Reverend Betts."

Betsy was right.

"I'll admit the will to probate."

I stood to leave.

"Do you have a legal problem, Sam?" He glanced up at me and smiled.

"No," I said, smiling back. "I just wanted to know if Springfield was as crowded as when I saw it a few years ago." I turned to leave.

"Can I tear up your messages?"

"You bet you can."

"Tell Betsy I said hello."

Bernie was fond of Betsy. Betsy and his late wife were close friends.

I walked out of his office past Jessie, standing up, and left.

***

That passage of realty to St. John the Baptist Church and Reverend Betts set Betsy thinking. She couldn't help but think about Norman. She thought he should stay on the farm, no matter who owned the property. He had lived in his shack on the Horner estate nearly ten years. The shack wasn't much, but it was his home and all he had. I'm sure he hadn't the money to buy or rent anything in or around town.

I tried to set aside any concern for him by placing his situation outside my official duties. After all, I was a lawman sworn to preserve law and order. Nevertheless, after my day ended in the office, I drove by the Horner estate to see him, satisfy my curiosity, and keep my promise to Betsy.

I pulled into the barnyard, with the treetops in the west tickling the belly of the sun. He walked out of the barn as I slammed shut the door of the county car. The years had worn the wood of the barn to a smoky gray color. He started to approach me, but I raised my hand for him to stop and walked over to the barn.

"How've you been, Norman?"

"Low, Sheriff Sam. Down low."

"Muriel was a good woman."

"She's in heaven. I know she's in heaven. She was always smilin', and she gave me them sweet cakes too."

I had nothing to say to that.

"I was on the back porch. I saw her through the screen door spread out on the kitchen floor. It was terrible. I didn't know what to do."

"Nobody could've done anything by then."

He just nodded.

We walked over to his shack. After he stepped inside, he stopped and looked back at me. When he saw me follow him, he eased up and walked over to his cot. After I sat on a chair by his table, he sat on the cot. The two of us sat in his shack for about a minute before he spoke.

"I don't see too much death, Sheriff Sam. I don't like death."

"Nobody likes death, Norman, but what can we do about it?"

He was sitting in the middle of the cot with his huge boots planted on the threadbare rug. He was rolling his big black callused hands over and over.

"I've been readin' the Good Book every night 'til I fall asleep."

He reached over and placed his hand gently on a worn black leather Bible setting on top of his pillow.

"I like the Good Book. I read the Book when I'm tired or sad or lonely, and I feel better. I do. I just do."

I couldn't say anything to that either.

"The Good Book says death is good. It says life comes from death. The Good Book says so. I'm lookin' for some good in all this death."

We fell silent again.

"I don't have the answers," I spoke up. "I really don't think anybody does. But it seems to me that you're looking in the right place."

Again, we fell silent. He was rolling big, simple thoughts over slowly in his mind. I could almost feel them rolling. I turned the conversation to the issues at hand. "Norman, have you been in the house yet?"

"No, sir. I've got my own place here."

"I suppose you'll be staying here for a while."

He didn't pick up the hint.

"I got to keep doin' the chores."

I let some time pass to approach him in a different way. "Do you know Reverend Betts?"

"He was Mrs. Horner's preacher, wasn't he?"

"That's right."

"I saw him a few times visitin' Mrs. Horner. He waved to me."

"He's a good man. I'll introduce you to him. You'll like him."

"I'd like that."

"I'll bring him by soon. How about that?"

"I'd like that just fine."

That was as close as I could get to telling him. I rose and walked to the door.

"Sheriff Sam?"

"Yes, Norman?"

"What's gonna happen to the farm now that Mrs. Horner's gone and all?"

I stopped for a moment. "We'll talk about that when I come back with the reverend. Until then, you keep up with those chores."

"You bet I will. I'm gonna take care of Mrs. Horner's farm."

I left with that. I couldn't say anything more. I didn't even know what was going to happen to him.

The trees were now traced in black by the sun. On my ride home, I felt a whole lot better for stopping. He seemed to be doing well in his own way.

I thought about him all the way home. The problem was peculiar. Almost everybody has read the Bible, at least parts of it. Scholars have studied the Bible for centuries. Preachers have been reciting it to people around the world. Here, in Greens Point, I found a lonely man using the Bible every night. Over dinner, I told Betsy about Norman and the Bible. She was pleased and not surprised one bit. She simply told me that the word comes alive when the mind *and* heart are opened. She emphasized *and* and pierced my eyes with those hazel eyes of hers.

"No matter what you say or do, there's still going to be mystery in life," she advised. "Neither your mind nor will can solve all of life's problems."

She didn't feel the need to say anything more.

Chapter 7

NOTHING big in life happens as planned. Life is mostly luck and timing, with a little hard work tossed in. That Wednesday was like most Wednesdays, midweek slow, not as hard as Mondays and not as easy as Fridays. Late morning was melting into a hot afternoon, a bellwether for the approaching summer.

Ever since the office meeting with my staff, Billy Ray was stopping too many drivers, and I was spending my afternoons apologizing on the telephone. Jeb was dodging Jessie. John had heard nothing in the lockup. Then again, nobody was arrested to be in the lockup. I had no need to call down Rusty. Hank was still chomping at the bit. Everything was proceeding according to plan. Nothing came up.

After a meat loaf sandwich with plenty of ketchup, I began my post-lunch walk on Main Street. In front of the general store, I noticed the pickup truck. Inside, I saw Lou behind the steering wheel. He looked a shade cleaner to me.

"Howdy, there," I called out.

"Sheriff," Lou called back.

"It looks like you ducked the rainstorm all right."

"That we did. We're just passing through again. We'll be on our way as soon as Duke comes out."

I saw the shovel and pick covered with mud in the truck bed. "Where are you two heading?"

"North, if the wheels hold out."

"What's up north?"

"I figure me and Duke might have better luck landing a job."

"I reckon. Our town doesn't have anything for types like you."

"I feel the same. We've had all we could take from your town just passing through it."

"Safe driving."

"Thanks."

Something wasn't setting right. I walked down the sidewalk a car length or two and then turned into Jeffries General Store. "Howdy, Clara."

"Sam."

Clara Jeffries was standing behind the cash register. She looked as neat and clean as she did any other day. The curls in her salt-and-pepper hair were pinned down tightly by black bobby pins. Duke was standing before her.

"Howdy, Duke."

Duke turned around. "Oh, Sheriff. Howdy to you too."

I stepped up next to him. "What are you buying?"

"Cigarettes for Lou and gum balls."

"Are the gum balls for you?"

"Yep."

He smiled, glaring down at the counter at three gum balls, red, blue, and green. He began to dig in his pocket for change. I heard Lou blast the truck horn.

"I'm takin' too long," he began to mumble out loud. "I got to hurry. Lou's gettin' mad." His big hand pulled out the contents of his pocket and slapped it on top of the counter. Amidst the change, I saw a gold pocket watch.

"Say there, Duke, aren't you somebody, a gold pocket watch."

I reached for the watch. "Do you mind if I take a look at it?" I picked up the watch.

"Sure, Sheriff."

"This watch looks like a fine ticker. It looks really old too. You can't buy a ticker like this one anymore."

"It's busted. I like to listen to it at night."

"Where did you get it?"

Duke paused. "Lou gave it to me."

"Where did he get it?"

Duke paused.

"I found it," Lou called over to us from the open doorway.

I was turning the watch over in my hand.

"Duke, ask the sheriff for your watch back. We got to get going."

"That's right, Sheriff. We got to get goin'. Can I have my watch back?"

"I'm afraid not."

Duke's wiry eyebrows arched. He immediately looked at Lou.

"J. T., J. T., J. T.," I said. "I'm trying to place those initials. The engraving on the watch says, 'J. T. B. C. Forever Roll.' If B. C. stands for Barge Company, then I'll bet my bottom dollar, and mind you I'm not a betting man, that J. T. stands for Jerome Taylor."

Lou quickly stepped in. "Sheriff, I found the watch. If you know this Jerome Taylor fellow and he's out a pocket watch, then you pass it on to him."

"No, Lou. I can't. You see, Jerome Taylor, who I believe owned a business called the Jerome Taylor Barge Company, has been dead for around a hundred years."

"You don't say. Ain't we lucky, me and Duke, finding that watch after all these years." Lou gave Duke a bump with his elbow and a big grin.

"Lucky," Duke mumbled as he tried to grin too.

Clara had stepped back from the counter. Through her eyes, I could tell the names and years tossed back and forth in the conversation were beginning to register.

"Hey, what's this all about anyhow? We ain't done nothing wrong. We're getting on our way." Lou reached for Duke's elbow.

I slowly pushed Lou's arm down. "Let's say you found the watch. But I'm not going to believe you found those brown shoes and belt, Lou."

"I ain't got to tell you when and where I buy my shoes, belt, or underwear. Let's get out of here, Duke."

"No, but you have to come to the office when I ask you. Let's go."

"We ain't going nowhere. You can't order us about. What are you taking us in for?"

"I want to talk to you fellows."

"What about?"

"Holy Hill Cemetery. You have some explaining to do."

"It ain't no crime buying some clothes."

"No, that's right. But digging up a grave for the clothes is."

Lou chuckled out a tight laugh. "What are you talking about? Let's go, Duke. We're leaving."

"Let's first walk across the street to my office. I just want to ask a few questions."

"You got it. Duke, let's make the lawman happy and stop in his office for a couple minutes."

The three of us left the general store, leaving the pack of cigarettes on the counter. After Clara picked out some coins, Duke scooped up the gum balls and change. Lou had his hands jammed in his pockets. Duke's arms dangled loosely at his sides.

When we entered my office, I was glad to find nobody inside. I walked over to my desk and sat. "Have a seat."

"Thanks," said Duke.

"Stand up, Duke," said Lou.

Duke froze.

"We ain't staying that long," continued Lou. "Fire your questions away."

"Now, Lou, correct me if I'm wrong, but I recall you wearing a rope tied around your waist when I saw you under the bridge."

Lou tapped Duke's arm. "See that. The lawman has a sharp memory. So what? What if I did?"

"Let's hold it a second. I have to tell you your rights."

I pulled out the top desk drawer. I kept a Miranda card somewhere inside the drawer.

"Forget it. I know my rights."

"No. If the courts want me to tell you these rights, then I'm going to do it. This won't take but a minute anyway, as soon as I find the card."

Lou gave Duke an elbow. "It seems like I was mistaken. We may be here a spell. We better pull up chairs. Down South here, I've noticed folks do things real slow."

Duke listened to Lou and sat. Lou jerked a chair beneath himself.

"You have a right to remain silent," I began. "You have a right to know that anything you say can and will be used against you in a court of law."

"What other kind of court is there?" Lou puffed out of the side of his mouth.

I kept on reading. "You have a right to have an attorney present during this questioning. If you cannot afford an attorney, you have a right to have an attorney appointed by the court."

"Let's get on with the questions. We've got places to go." Lou said.

Duke's eyebrows arched. "I heard all these before," he muttered. "We got places to go," he spoke up, glancing at Lou.

"That's right," I said with a chuckle, as I set the card down. "Lawyers just make more problems anyway."

"And charge you for it," Lou tossed in.

"Back to your belt. Where did it come from?"

"A store, where else?" Lou was grinning.

Duke smiled but tried to hold his laugh. He kept his eyes focused on his hands folded on his lap.

Lou, seeing Duke smile, gave him another elbow. "How about the lawman? He wants to know where my clothes come from. My shoes came from a store too. There. I tossed that one in for free."

"Thanks. I appreciate any cooperation you can show me. Now, did you buy the belt and shoes?"

"Sure. I ain't going to tell you, a lawman, I lifted them." Lou gave Duke the elbow again. Duke was still smiling.

"Where did you get them?"

"Across the river in Kentucky."

"Where in Kentucky?"

"Paducah."

"Where in Paducah?"

"Sheriff, what are you up to?"

"I just want to know the name of the store."

"I don't remember the name of the store."

I glanced at Duke. "Where did you get that watch, Duke?"

"Lou—" Duke began.

"We told you," Lou broke in.

I cut off Lou. "You do all the talking for Duke. Why don't you let him talk for himself?"

"I don't want any trouble. That's why. You lawmen twist up everything. I'm going to tell you something, lawman. Me and Duke, we travel together, see. We don't have much, never had, and maybe never will. But we got each other. I look out for Duke, and Duke helps me too. Maybe I talk better than Duke. So I do the talking. Maybe Duke's got bigger muscles. So Duke does the hauling. We're partners, me and Duke. And nobody, not even a lawman, is going to break us up unless I say so. Right, Duke?"

"Right, Lou. We're partners, you and me. You do the talkin', and I do the haulin'. Nobody's—"

"Okay, partner. I think the lawman got the point."

I leaned back in my desk chair and looked at Duke. He would not look at me. His eyes glanced around my desk and chair and then focused back on his hands on his lap. He was beginning to squeeze his hands.

"I only want Duke to tell me about the watch."

"Fine. Duke, did you hear the lawman? He only wants to know how I found the watch. Why don't you tell the lawman that?"

"That's right. Lou found the watch."

"Where did he find it?"

"He don't remember."

"I don't remember."

The two answered at the same time.

Hank walked into the office in his pushy and arrogant way. Although I always thought Hank had no judgment, I have to admit he looked like a lawman. That time, I was most pleased to see Hank's bulging biceps. "Hank, would you mind stepping over here?"

He did.

"Hank, would you mind showing these two fellows to the cells, separate, of course."

He stiffened up.

Lou jumped up out of his chair into Hank's grasp. Duke looked up.

"Sheriff, you had no right asking us questions. Now, you're tossing us in the slammer. What's the charge? I got the right to know that, don't I? What's the charge?"

"I'm calling it grave robbing, for starters, and probably theft. I can find the formal names for you later, if you'd like."

Lou's eyes rolled up to the ceiling as he belted out a roaring laugh. Duke remained sitting with his hands folded on his lap. He was looking up at Lou.

"Hank?"

Hank walked the two to the back room to the cells.

"I can't believe my ears," Lou hollered back. "This must be some kind of a small-town joke. But we'll play along with you—if the rooms come with meals."

He then belted out a howling laugh from the back room.

✻ ✻ ✻

With the suspects arrested, I had to turn my efforts to collecting evidence. I wanted statements but didn't want to drag in any attorney to foul up my approach. Bernie Cain was down the street, and Tony Pinelli, the public defender of Clermont County, and his assistant public defenders were a stone's throw away in the courthouse.

Consequently, I figured the problem out as such: I would first confront Lou, the bold one. From the first time we met, I noticed Lou was the boss and ran Duke. If I called out Duke first, Lou might holler for an attorney to protect Duke. If I called out Lou first, his pride would guide us around attorneys into statements.

Acting on better judgment and my gut feelings, I had Hank take Lou out of the cell. I also asked Hank then to keep an eye on Duke. I felt there was no need for Hank to cuff Lou to the chair or to watch my approach to Lou. I didn't want anybody looking over my shoulder. After Hank walked back to the cells, I began to talk to Lou. "Lou, I want to talk to you alone, so as not to worry or confuse your buddy."

Lou wasn't as boisterous after having been led to the cell. He was just staring at me.

"The courts say I can't make any promises, so I'm not. But the courts do see fit to go easier on fellows who cooperate with the system. But I suspect you're rather familiar with the system."

He drew a slow smile across his lips.

"The courts go much easier on fellows who cooperate and aren't too familiar with the system, like your friend. Do you read me?"

His eyes opened a twitch wider.

"Good. I'm glad we're understanding each other."

I walked over to the coffee pot. "Coffee?"

He shook his head.

I filled a mug for myself and eased back in my chair. I leaned the chair back against the wall. "The way I see it, you and your buddy will be going down in front of any jury in Clermont County. Let's look at the important points. First, grave poaching is despicable and likely to raise the passions of any reasonable community, let alone Greens Point. Second, out-of-towners, especially drifters, aren't taken to too kindly down here."

He rolled his eyes.

"The prosecutor, Bob Hunt, with any jury, could take you down right quick. And mind you now, I haven't even begun talking about the evidence. Down here in the southern counties, appeals move a bit slower too. Most offenders realize they'll be walking long before their appeals are heard. Let me see, how can I say it? Appeals aren't too important down here."

He stared off over my left shoulder.

"And last, you have to look at the evidence against you. We have you two carrying Jerome Taylor's watch and wearing the belt and shoes of Henry Albrecht. A juror doesn't have to take too big a leap to infer you pulled them out of the graves."

His stare switched over my right shoulder.

"Of course, I can't say I exactly measured Mr. Albrecht's feet and waist for proof positive. But then again, no juror in Greens Point would forgive me for digging up the grave already once violated. No, Bob will probably ask me on the witness stand my opinion on the approximate size of Mr. Albrecht. I'd have to say Mr. Albrecht did look about as short and thin as you. And in case you forgot, Mr. Albrecht's burial suit was brown, like those shoes and belt. Since I'm speaking about evidence now, would you kindly slip off those shoes and belt?"

His stare aimed right back at me.

"Now," I commanded.

He bent forward and untied and kicked off the brown shoes. After he straightened up, he unbuckled and pulled off the brown belt.

"Before I call the prosecutor, would you like to tell me anything?"

He remained silent.

"Coffee?"

He nodded.

I stood, poured a mug, and handed it over to him. He sipped the hot black coffee.

"Do you mind if I smoke?" Lou asked.

I shook my head.

He pulled a crumpled pack of cigarettes and worn paper matchbook from his shirt pocket. He tapped out a cigarette, lit it, and drew a couple long, hard hits from it before he began to talk.

"Sheriff, you crossed the wrong man. See, I've got you in a corner," he said. He sipped his coffee, waiting for me to respond.

"Explain yourself."

"You've been talking plea bargain," he said.

"I couldn't have said it any clearer myself."

"What you don't understand is I've got nothing but time and nowhere to go. You don't have much leverage when you're pressing me with nothing more than time for grave poaching and theft."

I gave him my steady make-or-break stare and waited a moment. "I'm not doing any time. You are."

74

"You're in store for a hell of a lot worse," he shot right back at me. "On the witness stand in court, I can draw the worst attention to Greens Point that has ever fallen on the town. If I'm going down, I'm taking you and everybody else in this poky little town with me."

I played deadpan and let him go on.

"In court, I can tell my story, and you can tell yours. I might tell those jurors I told you we dug up those graves. I might also say I was throwing you the biggest line of bullshit I could imagine. Don't forget, only me and you know what we're saying now."

I remained silent.

"If I testify," he continued, "your town will never be the same. I can drop the biggest bomb on this town in the town's—no country's—history. You and your town will be the butt end of the biggest joke ever dropped in court. So you give that some long hard thought."

I sipped my coffee. I felt a bit like a bear cornered by four traps with three directions to walk. "I read that as a threat."

"I figured even a lawman can read."

"I'll be darned. I get a kick out of you out-of-towners. I've never been threatened by a prisoner before today."

"I know you're going to run my sheet. So what? I'll save you some time. See, I'm cooperating with the system. You'll learn I've been in the joint. So what? You can send me back, maybe, probably—so what? Before you arrested me, I didn't have a roof over my head. I didn't eat regular meals. Now, I've got a roof, a bed, and daily meals. You've got a roof, a town, and a public office. I can send you down the river."

I took a deep breath to slow the pace down. His running at the mouth wasn't helping me. I tried a different tack.

"Who cares about Clermont County?" I asked Lou.

"When I'm done testifying, I'd say the state of Illinois and maybe even the whole country."

"We're down here in Clermont County." I tried to bluff. "I can't see any big-shot reporters poking their heads around here."

"Sheriff."

"Go on."

"You can't hide. Your types call me a 'criminal.' I know all about hiding out. If this town puts me on trial, the town is going to be put on trial. Nobody will be able to hide. Nothing will be hidden. If you all hold me up as a criminal during the trial, I'll show off the true colors of everybody in

75

this backward little river town. You people living in these small towns aren't the simple Holy Rollers you lead the big-city people to believe. It could be time for a shake-up. And I could be the shaker."

I had already finished my coffee. I guess I was thirsty. I rose, poured myself another mug, and sat again. He handed me a half-full mug.

"Could you warm it up for me?" he asked, cracking a sliver of a smile.

I had no other choice under the circumstances. I went and warmed his mug.

I raised my hand. "Stop here for a moment. I'm being nice to you. I can't see one reason for your attack."

"No attack. Not now. Not yet." He puffed away at his cigarette.

I kept sipping coffee, trying to cipher a plan of attack. I couldn't come up with another indirect approach. "Did you dig up those graves?"

He shot back a sharp response. "What's the answer going to get me?"

"Leniency."

"Wrong answer."

I stood up and walked over to the gun rack. "We don't play guessing games here in Clermont County."

"Back off. This case is going to be tried. You're an elected official. An elected official will always pass the buck to twelve unelected jurors. Politicians don't do what they think is right. They do whatever will keep them in office."

"You're losing my interest," I said.

"Come on. If a jury decides a man's fate, 'the people' have spoken. The jury made your decision. You're safe. On top of all that doing nothing, you get all that press. You've got nothing to lose and everything to gain in trying me."

It was at this stage of the interrogation of the suspect that I realized Lou was no Tommy Sparks. Lou had an ax to grind against society. Unfortunately, I represented society.

I'm not saying he was telling all lies. But then again, I'm not saying he was telling the whole truth. As an elected official in the peaceful town of Greens Point, I actually preferred to keep a jury and the press out of the matter. Nevertheless, I had sworn to uphold the duties of my office wherever they took me—whether that be on the witness stand or before the reporter's pen.

"I don't need to hear your problems with the system," I said, shaking my head.

Again, I tried a direct attack. "Did you dig up those graves?"

"No."

I had been a lawman too long to rest on that answer. "You were there, though, when Duke dug up the graves?"

He pushed his mug on my desk toward me. "Warm it up again," he said.

I grabbed the mug and noticed he hadn't taken a sip. I figured he was stalling. I dripped a little hot coffee into the mug to give him a few more moments to think and set it back on my desk.

"Sheriff, I'm going to make you a deal. How do you like that?"

"Let me hear what you have to say first."

"All right. I might just confess that Duke and I robbed those graves. Or I could tell you I found the watch. I could say I picked the belt and shoes out of somebody's trash. I could also tell you that I bought the belt and shoes. Without a job, though, that's hard for you and, later, the jury to swallow."

He looked up at the ceiling.

"How about stole them? That's closer to my types, right?"

His eyes dropped down at me. "Where? When? I could have easily lifted them from shops across the river in Paducah than dug up graves. Shoplifting makes more sense than grave digging. A jury could go for that simple conclusion. A jury might even go quicker for that if I admit it to you in this confession you're trying to extract out of me."

He took another hit from his cigarette. "But if I hit that witness stand, I might very well tell that jury that everything I told you was a joke. Got that, Sheriff? A joke. I got the power to make you the punch line of the biggest whopper that ever hit your county. Then we'll see how long your career lasts."

"I doubt if our jurors will take to your sense of humor."

"I got nothing to lose. You got money. I don't. Society likes you, not me. You and your types pushed me down lower than your cats and dogs. Before you arrested me, I didn't know when my next meal would come. So you might say I climbed out from the gutter and into the grave—not much of a step. If I didn't, I'd be in my grave right now. Of course, you and your types can't understand that."

I stopped him. "Lou, isn't there a limit to a man's acts?"

"Sheriff, I'm at a point you'll never know. No. I act. That's all. I do—without rules. See, rules ain't been too good to me. My only rule is that there are no rules. I don't follow rules. The only rules are your rules. Why should I use them?"

"Because it's the law," I answered.

"You just don't understand. After a man's been beaten down for years by rules, he doesn't use rules."

I cocked my head to the side.

"If I say to you that I raided the graves, so? So I could get jewelry to pawn and have some fun in life, like you folks? Everybody's got a right to have some fun. I had fun in Kentucky. I drank real whiskey. I laughed without any worries for a few hours. Maybe I even bought me and Duke a gift or two. That ain't much, is it? Corpses can't use gold. A man can. Gold's for the living. Gold can buy fun. Nobody was hurt. The corpses sure weren't hurt."

I pinched the bridge of my nose. I had run into some sort of problem even Hank's law enforcement magazines couldn't help me solve. I realized I needed particulars in any confession I could get. I had to know the details of the diggings that only the offender would know. After the general complaints he flung at me, I felt he would bare the details. At that stage in my investigation, I set aside his courtroom bomb threat to cross at a later time. I tried again. "What about the graves?"

"Hold on. I got more to say. I'll tell you anything you want to hear about the graves. Let me try to set your mind straight first."

He drew a final, deep drag from his cigarette butt before he spoke. "My entire life's been running from the gutter down to the sewer. I'm that nobody that you, the jock, and the president of the high school class never—and I mean never—talked to. If you had talked to my types in high school, you might have been able to see what you and me would become."

I sat still. I wanted to keep the prisoner talking and didn't want him to clam up.

"Let me tell you about the other side of the tracks—and for my life that ain't just a saying. I was raised in Harvey, due south on the Illinois Central tracks one hour out of Chicago. Harvey was a thriving south suburb, but it faded fast as its factories closed. All of the hardworking laborers who made the executives rich had been turned out on the street with the crunch in heavy industry. Most of the executives saw the fall coming, and they pulled out. Nobody warned the workers.

"I used to ride freight trains to and from high school when the trains were passing. There was something in those big, greasy iron wheels turning over and over that pulled me up to the tracks but scared the pants off the proper boys in high school. I spent my Saturdays laying pennies on the tracks ahead of the freight trains. I hid as the trains rolled over the pennies. After the freighter passed, I rushed up onto the tracks and searched for the pennies in the limestone railbed.

"Lincoln's face was squashed into all sorts of funny shapes. The good boys who'd talk to me paid at least a nickel and sometimes a quarter for the pennies with the deformed heads. The good girls who'd look would squinch up their noses and turn away in a huff. I only had those pennies to offer them. I didn't have the money or use for an ID bracelet or class ring. As a high school hoodlum, I was running quite a racket."

I nodded at him to continue.

"High school was a big farce. The dean of boys thought he was the Genghis Khan of the high school. He was the frustrated ball player who never made it big to the major league. He got passed up, so he took it out on students like me who had no plans. What teenager has real plans?

"Whenever I got caught cutting classes, smoking in the john, or taking a sip of whiskey from a half pint I kept stashed in my locker, that henchman suspended me. Of course, the suspension hinged on my parents coming to school and meeting with him. My father was dead. My mother worked in the only factory still open after huge layoffs. I never asked her to take a day off to talk to him. Anyhow, she wouldn't have gone. I was suspended. My ma never knew because she was either sleeping or working whenever I was home. My favorite dinner was white bread dipped in broiled meat pan drippings and salt. I can see and taste them now.

"In other words, when I stepped out of line, I was whacked. I was whacked right out of high school. The jocks' hands were never even tapped. High school jocks are a select few. My brow was beaten twice as hard to cover for the lectures aimed at correcting their mistakes."

"Don't try to hide your problems behind excuses," I said.

He slapped the desktop. "Excuses? What do you think the jocks' parents lay on the schools? High school athletes don't get in trouble. Come on."

"Let's just say I'm not familiar with your school district."

He threw a hand up in my face. "It doesn't stop in high school. I never saw my ma all week. She was too busy earning a lousy living in a sweaty factory and drinking cold beer down at the corner tavern after work. After I dropped out of high school, I moved out."

"You could have found a job."

"Stop. I don't want to hear that establishment crap. I found jobs, gas stations and car washes. Those ain't career jobs. I made money when I could. I moved on after a few months. Of course, you can't understand that."

"Maybe."

"I worked and drifted. I'll tell you now I drifted more than I worked. I drifted away from home to warmer climates. And what did I find?"

I had no answer.

"And what did I find? I'll tell you. Nothing. As a child, I heard about boxcar bums. I even saw a few. When I was a teenage know-it-all, I pelted stones at one who hid in an empty boxcar. You can't imagine how I felt the first night I slept in an empty boxcar. Warnings, plans, dreams—all are crushed the first night in an empty boxcar.

"And it didn't get better. I slept under trees at night in the rain. Even pet dogs got a roof over their heads. I pulled a flimsy jacket over me and rolled myself up into a ball. I still got soaked. I've lived like a wild animal on the outskirts of town."

There wasn't much I could say.

"That's it. I took some hard knocks. I did what I could and survived. It might have been in boxcars and the brush, but I survived."

I tried again to discuss the graves. "I'm not saying you haven't had it bad. But why the graves? Why the graves?"

"Why? Why not? What's the difference to a man who can't even afford a grave? Society chewed me up and spit me out. I don't operate like you and your types. I got no money, no job, and no hope."

He dropped his head for a few seconds. "So the graves were dug up," he continued. "Big deal. Nobody was hurt. The gold was put to use. You just don't understand. Nothing matters . . . nothing matters."

He slowly shook his head and looked down at his hands folded together on his lap.

I let a minute pass before attempting again to refocus my interrogation. "Tell me about the graves."

"Okay. Since you might be the punch line, you ought to hear the joke. I told Duke to dig, and he dug. The first was as easy as the last. Duke was tired. It was way past his bedtime. Duke ain't no night owl. He was in dreamland. Duke was confused. I told him to act like it was Halloween. I convinced him we were playing a trick. And you know Duke. He'll say or do anything I want. Next morning, I told Duke that he was dreaming. Now, Duke thinks he was dreaming. So I let him think so. Thinking so doesn't hurt him any."

I raised my eyebrows and said, "Duke's your right arm."

"Don't you start up on Duke. I met him in Joliet. We got out of jail about the same time. He had no place to go. Your types just turn them out on the street. But I couldn't see that big lug going off alone. He doesn't have the smarts to last a week. I said, 'Duke, come along with me a bit, and we'll see how it works out.' Let me tell you, lawman, he was as happy as a puppy to have someone look after him.

"Duke's ma died while he was in the joint with me. When I met him in jail, he had no past to speak of and no future. So we traveled together. Sure, I'm hard on him at times, but I ain't been no harder than the foster homes he was raised in. We traveled through the Midwest and South together. Duke, he ain't never traveled. He loved every day of it. When I needed to, but not too often, I threatened to leave him, and he straightened out real quick.

"I showed him towns, farms, and rivers. I showed him freedom he'd never known. I was hard on him, but I protected that dumb lug. Me and him are like brothers. I never let nobody take a swing at him because he could kill 'em with one punch. Whenever we had an extra can of beans, I'd give him it all. He's just an overgrown kid. Duke—dumb as he is—he's the best friend anybody could ever have."

I picked up on his lead. "So why did you make him dig up the graves?"

"Why?" Lou leaned back in his chair. He let out a slow broad smile. "Why? I told you why. He doesn't know any better than what I tell him. He just says or does what I tell him. And don't you get any lawman ideas in your head. If he now thinks he was dreaming, let him think so. He doesn't know about any grave robbing. So see, lawman, the joke is still on you."

"Do you mind me asking about the gold?"

"Like we said, I found it."

"You found it on the bodies?"

"Suit yourself. You're going to write your reports how you want to. You don't need me."

"Two corpses were rifled through pretty badly. I figure you made off with a haul of gold, silver, and jewelry."

"Yeah, I found some gold and pawned it. We had it decent for a day or two."

"What about the gold watch?"

"To keep Duke happy, I gave him the J. T. watch. That stupid giant, he slept every night with the watch tucked under his head next to his ear. It's busted, but he thinks it ticks. So what? Does it really matter? We ain't got no use for time. Time hasn't been good to us. He falls asleep listening to it tick. It makes him happy. Wait until you see him smile. Lawman, you'll let him keep the watch when you see how he smiles at it."

"Did Duke use the shovel and pick in your truck bed?"

"Those are the only big tools we got."

We sat silently for about a minute.

"I think that's enough for now," I said. "Why don't you turn in?"

"I could use some sleep."

We stood up.

"Hank," I called.

Before Hank came out of the lockup, Lou turned toward me. "Be easy on Duke," he said. "He's nothing but a big kid. Try not to scare him. If you decide that wrong's been done, I've done it all. He's got no bad in his heart. If he does, I put it there. He's only a kid."

I gave Lou a small smile.

Hank walked out of the lockup.

"Hank, take Lou back and bring out Duke."

I followed Hank and Lou back to the lockup.

"Duke," I heard Lou say. "You can talk to the sheriff. He won't hurt you."

I looked into the big fellow's eyes, and he smiled.

Chapter 8

"Is it my turn to talk to the sheriff?" Duke asked.

"It sure is," I said.

Lou shook his head as he walked into his cell to sit on the bunk. After Hank locked the cell door, I called back to him.

"Hank, do me another favor, would you? Bring the shovel and pick from the truck bed into the office?"

After Hank left, I sat down behind my desk. "Sit down. Coffee?"

"No, sir. Lou don't like me to drink coffee or booze. I can't sleep if I drink it. My legs keep rockin' back and forth."

"Mind if I have a cup?"

"Course not, Sheriff. You're the sheriff."

I stood up to warm up my mug. He sat there watching me. He had a slight grin. Maybe he thought this was all a game. He must have felt proud, too, to get the go-ahead from Lou.

I sat down across from him. He had a frame as huge as Norman's. His stubbly beard was a shade or two of red lighter than his dark red, almost brown hair, cropped short and brushed straight back. His thick, wiry eyebrows matched his hair. His hair matched his freckles and big passive eyes. His sleeveless gray sweatshirt, worn inside out, revealed his massive arms.

"It's good to see you again, Duke."

"Same here."

"But this time, we get to talk a bit more."

"Lou says so?"

"You heard him. Lou says so."

I detected a big, lonely heart under that huge frame. He strove to speak like Lou and other adults. I recognized he was likely an outcast from his childhood onward. No matter how he appeared not to be hurt, he'd been hurt, lost, and lonely, wandering within himself, with no friends but Lou.

"Where are you from?"

"Joliet, Illinois."

He pronounced the city *Jolly-et*.

"That's southwest of Chicago, right?" I asked.

"It's where the big prison is."

Again, I remembered. I began to feel a little bit guilty trying to talk him into a confession. "I have to ask you about the times you dug for Lou."

His nostrils twitched slightly. His head lowered.

"I have to ask these questions. It's my job," I said gently.

His eyes were still downcast.

"All right. Do you remember doing some digging with Lou?"

"Yep, I remember diggin', but I was dreamin'."

"Let's not get into any dreaming right now. I want you to tell me about the digging."

He gave me a blank stare.

"Lou told you where to dig, didn't he?"

"Yep."

I kept pausing and moving slowly with him. I didn't want to scare or lose him. "You dug three times, didn't you?"

"Three."

"What did you use?"

"The shovel and pick in the truck."

I saw him glance at the shovel and pick Hank had set down against the wall by my desk.

"These?" I pointed to the shovel and pick.

"Yep." He still wouldn't look at me.

"How deep did you dig?"

"I dug 'til Lou told me to stop."

I slowed down even more. "Weren't you digging up graves?"

"I was just diggin'."

I eased up. "What did you do when Lou told you to stop?"

"I stopped. Lou never steered me wrong."

"Then what did you do?"

"I climbed out of the holes."

"How deep were the holes?"

"Deep."

"What did Lou do?"

He looked up. "I don't know," he said. "I walked off and found myself a place to sit, like Lou told me. I rested. I heard him climb in the holes, though, and some rustlin' too."

I stopped for a sip of coffee. "What were you two doing?"

He looked up into my eyes with blank eyes. "Lou said it was a secret," he said.

"But he told you to talk to me, didn't he?"

"Yep, he did."

Duke looked like he was rolling a big thought over in his mind. "He said we was playin' a trick, like Halloween."

"Who was the trick being played on?"

"I don't know. He never told me."

"Didn't you ask him?"

"I don't ask him much."

The whole time we talked about the trick, he kept glancing out of the sides of his eyes like a child hiding something. I felt he was beginning to break through his dream. Perhaps the nights were coming back to him. I had a hunch he might have known what they were up to, but he either didn't tell Lou he knew or he wouldn't now tell me. I pressed him for some answers.

"Weren't you two stealing from a graveyard?"

"Lou made no mention of stealin'."

"Well, he gave you a gold watch."

"He told me he found it."

"He found it in one of the coffins?"

"I never seen no coffin."

I changed directions. "Let me ask you about something else for a while, okay?"

"Okay."

"You and Lou came into some money across the Ohio in Paducah, right?"

"We came into some money."

"How much?"

"I don't know. He never showed me it all. He keeps the money in his pockets, sometimes his shoe."

"Where'd he get the money?"

"Across the Ohio in Paducah."

"No. I mean, where in Paducah did he get the money?"

"Oh, that's easy. He got the money in a pawn shop, he called it. It looked like an old jewelry store to me."

"How'd he get it?"

"He sold the gold jewelry."

"What jewelry?"

"The jewelry . . . " he paused, "Lou found."

"Where did he find it?"

Duke was slowing down with his answers. "I don't know. He said he found it in different places. He's up all night."

"What did he find?"

"He showed me cufflinks and rings. He gave me the gold watch."

"Anything else?"

"Nope, just things like that."

I slipped to another area. "How about clothes?" I asked him.

"What kind?" he asked.

"Did he ever show you a belt and shoes?"

"I saw a belt and shoes on him in Paducah."

"Did you see where he got them?"

"Nope."

"Did he tell you where he got them?"

"He said he wished they were bigger so I could wear them."

"That was nice of him to say."

Duke smiled and nodded. "Lou's nice to me. He watches out for me. Sometimes, he tries to teach me things or tell me things I should say or do. But I mostly forget them or don't understand them. I try, though. I try as hard as I can."

"I'm sure you do."

He was still smiling. I thought I'd set him up pretty well.

"Duke," I said.

He looked at me.

"Did Lou find the jewelry in the holes you dug?"

He paused. His eyes slowly turned upward. "I was dreamin' 'bout them holes," he said.

He bluntly slammed the door on my inquiry. I moved to another area. "Let me ask you about something else."

"Okay."

"What were you two going to do with the money Lou was keeping?"

"We was gonna buy us some roots."

"What do you mean by 'buy us some roots'?"

"I don't know for sure. Lou told me that at night when we were tired of driftin'. He said I could have the pocket watch 'til we bought us some roots."

"What else did he tell you?"

He smiled and started to rock back and forth in his seat as he recalled. "He told me driftin' ain't good for nobody. He'd tell me how we were gonna set up near Joliet but farther southwest, in a smaller town. I told him I wanted to go home. He didn't want to be too close to a city, though. He said I'd get myself in trouble in a city. He talks like that a lot. I like listening to him, 'specially by a campfire."

"What would you do at the campfire?"

"I'd listen 'til my eyelids wouldn't stay open. Then I'd lay on my side and curl my arm under my head with my pocket watch in the palm of my hand, so I could listen for the ticks. I kept thinkin' 'bout not driftin', 'bout havin' my own bed. I was gonna do all the liftin' and haulin'. He was gonna do all the talkin' and thinkin'. We was gonna go into business."

He smiled as he drifted off. I'd never seen a smile quite like his. It was the most painful I'd ever seen.

"So you guys were going to set up a business?"

"Yep. We was gonna go into business, so we could be our own bosses."

"What kind of business?"

His smile was still spread. "A corner tap. We was gonna open a corner tap for anybody to come in. Lou said we'd call it Duke's. I like that, Duke's. Do you like that Sheriff, Duke's?"

"I can't think of a better name." I caught myself starting to drift off with him. "Can we go back to the digging for a bit?" I asked.

His smile snapped. He looked down into his big hands.

"Do you remember how many nights you dug?"

"I don't remember how many dreams I had."

"I'm not asking you how many dreams about digging you remember. I'm asking you how many diggings you remember."

His nose squinched up.

"How many times did Lou tell you to dig? Three, wasn't it?"

"Three."

"Where did you dig?"

"I don't remember."

"Lou told you where to dig?"

He nodded.

I eased back in my chair and reached into my pants pocket.

"Duke, when did Lou give you this?"

I slid the gold pocket watch over the desktop in front of him. His face lit up.

"He gave me that in Paducah."

He reached for it but then stopped and looked up at me.

"I'm sorry. I can't give it back to you."

"I was figurin' so."

He pulled his hands and eyes back onto his lap. His shoulders slumped.

I paused. "You just hold on for a moment."

I turned around in my chair, leaned over, and pulled a cardboard box setting by the trash can over to my chair. I sifted through the official lost and found box.

"Here. Take it. It's yours."

I slid a wrist watch with no wrist band over to him and pulled back the pocket watch as I slid my hand back.

"Go on, pick it up."

He did, cautiously. The watch looked fragile as a peanut shell in his paws.

"It's a real watch, just like the pocket watch, but it doesn't tell time."

"I don't care 'bout the time. I like to hear the ticks at night."

"That's why I'm giving it to you. But be careful with it now. Before you go to bed at night, you wind the little knob up no more than ten times. You don't want to bust it. Then each night, you can listen to the ticks."

A tiny smile began to break on his face. "Thanks. I'll be real careful with it. You want me to keep it for you?"

"No. It's yours. I had to take the pocket watch."

He slid the watch carefully into his pants pocket where he had kept the pocket watch. He patted that pocket and smiled.

"Okay. You want to talk some more?"

He just nodded. I could tell he was still thinking about his new watch.

"Lou showed you the jewelry in the morning in Paducah?"

"Yep."

"He showed you cufflinks and rings?"

"And a tack he said was for ties."

"Were they gold?"

"Yep, Lou said so."

"He sold them for cash across the river?"

He nodded. He rubbed his thigh where the watch was tucked into his pants pocket.

"You don't know how much money he got for them, do you?"

"Nope."

"What did you two do with the money?"

"First, we bought us a square meal. Lou had some kind of steak. I had meat loaf and mashed potatoes and gravy."

"Did you buy anything else?"

"Lou bought whiskey. He just laid around a couple of days, drinkin', laughin', and sleepin'."

"Did you buy anything else?"

"Gas for the truck."

"Anything else?"

"Nope. That was 'bout all we bought."

"Did you have any money left?"

His eyes just opened wide at mine, indicating that he probably didn't know or no.

I decided I had enough evidence to charge them at least with possession of stolen property. I figured that, if I pushed him for more details, I'd only confuse him.

"Sheriff, how long are you keepin' Lou and me here?"

I took a long breath. "That's hard to say. But it looks like I'm going to have to book you and Lou."

His head dropped. "I was figurin' so. Lou will see us through all this. He takes care of me. I've known Lou for four years, and he takes care of him and me."

"Lou told me he met you way back in Joliet."

"Yep. We met in Joliet. Lou was doin' time for burglary. I was in for car theft. But I was just the passenger. My mom, she died while I was in jail. Some lawyer sent me a note after the burial tellin' me no money was left after expenses and his fees. She had nothin' anyway." He rubbed the wells around his eyes. "I never did nothin' worse than let my mom die alone. Nobody should ever die alone. I never got to say goodbye to her."

Duke's mind was slipping to the past fast. I tried to retrieve it. "So it's been Lou and you ever since then?"

"Yep. We been partners. I got nobody but Lou. People get mad at me sometimes 'cause I'm slow at learnin' things. Lou does too. But he says he yells at me to help me. He doesn't give up on me. I don't learn so fast."

"But you have more muscle than two or three men put together."

He smiled and nodded. "That's why Lou and me are good partners. I got the muscles, and Lou's got the brains."

"Duke, how long did you dig?" I tried to catch him off guard.

"'Til I seen them tunnels to heaven."

"Tunnels to what?"

"Heaven. White clouds risin' up through the tree branches."

"Oh, you mean the morning mist."

He didn't even hear me. "Mama used to call them tunnels to heaven." He was staring off to a place I'd never been to.

"Go ahead and wind your watch."

He looked up at me, then stood up, following me. "No more than ten times," he said.

I nodded.

"Hank," I called.

Hank came out for Duke.

"Show Duke to his cell."

I sat down again and pulled out a drawer for an official report form. Before I began to write summaries of their statements, I ran through both of the conversations in my mind.

After locking Duke back up, Hank walked across the room to the door. I could tell he was perturbed at me for my asking him to sit by the cells while I interrogated each prisoner.

"Thanks, Hank."

He stopped.

I knew I should have let him go to blow off his steam.

"Thanks for what? For babysitting? I didn't work hard for this badge to babysit prisoners."

"Don't go blowing things out of proportion. There was only two of us and two of them. They had to be separated. Besides, I'd seen the graves."

I figured I'd hit a soft spot, but I hoped to avoid a full-blown argument. Like I said before, Hank and Bob Hunt were off on a fishing trip when I discovered the robbed graves at Holy Hill.

"You've taken statements, fine," Hank said. "Did you reduce those statements to signed written confessions?"

I only kept my stare on him.

"Are you going to develop some scientific evidence, soil samples or fingerprints?" he asked.

I leaned forward in my chair.

"First off, Deputy. I don't have to answer to anybody but the voters of Clermont County. Second, you read too many magazines. Those law enforcement magazines are starting to control your mind instead of your mind controlling them. Third, we're not in Chicago, New York, or Los Angeles. We don't have their resources. We don't need their resources because we don't have their crime and we don't face their juries. Fourth, goodbye, Hank."

He stormed out.

I turned to writing the summaries and wound up taking twice as long writing them as taking them. My official reports would serve as the basis for the people of the State of Illinois to formally charge Lou Vitale and Raymond "Duke" Samms.

Chapter 9

"I T's about time we talked," I said. "My case is closed. You can pick up my reports and the evidence, so you can charge them. I'll be in all morning."

I hung up the telephone. Bob Hunt, the state's attorney of Clermont County, was upset. I hadn't called for his assistance. Like Hank, Bob got rankled when he didn't get a piece of the action. Regardless of their egos, I was the elected sheriff of Clermont County. I had a hunch at the time. Besides, Hank was out after my elected office. I wasn't going to help him push me out of a job. Bob said he'd been trying to call me. But with Jeb ailing with that rheumatism, I explained that I wasn't getting phone messages.

The mayor of Greens Point, Jethro P. Stubbs, was an altogether different story. So long as the culprits ran loose, he wouldn't come near the investigation or even comment on it in the *Bugler*. The unsolved investigation was mine, and he didn't want to interfere—or so he said. But the very day after the arrest, he called. He wanted some press from the arrests. Just one photograph of Mr. Mayor would cover the front page. I wasn't too anxious to have a photograph of him and me on the front page, with me pressed along the margin and Mr. Mayor consuming pretty near the whole frame, no matter what angle or lens the photographer used. Out of respect, I called and politely skirted his hints. I'm certain he took my avoidance personally. He had some notion I wanted to be mayor.

Pursuant to my duty, I met with the county prosecutor on the morning following the arrests and interrogations of Lou and Duke. I poured us some mugs of coffee.

"What do you have for me?" he asked.

"Proceeds, statements, and tools of the crime," I replied.

He tried not to act angry or impressed.

"Let me see what you have."

Across my desktop, I shoved my summaries of the statements. I pulled open my top desk drawer and slid over the pocket watch too.

"The shovel and pick are in the back hallway."

Again, he looked at me coolly. I'm sure he was fuming inside. Of all the weeks to take off fishing with Hank, it just so happened the biggest crime hit Clermont County. Consequently, I had had to clear the case without his help. On my own, I had recovered physical evidence and obtained statements.

Bob wasn't the brightest lawyer I had ever met. He was the type of fellow who looked like his intelligence. His thin blond hair was balding in front. His forehead stood out flatly and bluntly above his eyes. His dull blue eyes never fully focused, no matter what I ever told him. Caught off guard, he wore a blank, gaping expression on his face.

Nevertheless, he worked hard. What he didn't carry upstairs, he packed in his heart. No county could have a more hard-driving prosecutor.

He raised his head from my report. "Where are the written confessions?"

"I didn't take any."

"Did you collect any soil samples from the pick and shovel?"

"No, the mud's still on them, but it's dry now."

If I had closed my eyes and he had changed his voice, I would have sworn Hank was sitting in front of me.

Bob stopped asking questions. I suppose he didn't want to become too obvious.

The front door flew open. Mayor Stubbs barely squeezed through it. He kind of kicked his feet out in front of him as he walked over to my desk. He was wearing a powder-blue suit, white shirt open at the collar, and a wide-brimmed white hat with a navy blue band. His cheeks were flushed. His red face and blue suit made his blue eyes stand out. Everybody's proud of at least one part of their body. He took off his hat and wiped the sweat from his brow with a navy blue-and-white paisley-print hanky.

"Do we got the goods on those grave robbers?"

Probably from his size, he wasn't shy to butt right into a situation.

"We've got proceeds, statements, and the tools they used," I answered.

"Guilty," he said, as he patted the tips of his fingers together on top of his belly.

He bit his lip, squirted out a surprised look on his face, and began bouncing out a chuckle.

"Here, Mayor, I'll let you read my report," I said. I picked the report up off my desk and held it out to him.

He held up his hand. "Bob, you're the prosecutor. What do they say?"

"I have enough to charge them," Bob answered.

"That's enough. That's all you have to tell me."

Mayor Stubbs looked back at me. "Where's the evidence?" he asked.

Even though boys grow up to become adults, they still like to play cops and robbers whenever they get a chance.

I pointed to the pocket watch on my desk.

He sat himself down on a chair before my desk.

"Proceeds," I said.

"Ah, the proceeds," echoed the mayor.

"Night two or three, grave number two or three. J. T. Jerome Taylor."

"What else do you have to show me?" he asked.

"Wait here," I answered. I walked to the back hallway to retrieve the tools. I carried them over to rest them up against my desk. He pulled his knee with his hand in closer away from the dirty tools.

"Anything else?" he asked.

"What else do you need?" I answered. "The defendants are back in the lockup."

"What's next?"

"You'll have to ask Bob that question. I was elected to preserve law and order throughout our county. On my part, I have restored law and order. We, here in Clermont County, were set back by an unforeseen crime. I met the task and arrested the culprits."

Bob was looking off somewhere else. Mayor Stubbs was intently gazing at me, rubbing the tips of his fingers gently under his nose. He did that often when he was thinking. He was probably smelling the garlic on his fingertips.

"Is this your reelection speech, Sheriff?"

"I'm undecided on another term as sheriff. I'd be more than glad and downright pleased if you'd use it as part of your State of the Town speech."

The mayor tooted out a breath through his nostrils and dropped his hand to his thigh.

Bob took a pass on the defendants. Mayor Stubbs took a peek at them as he left. By waiting out the problem and letting it work itself out, with a little luck, my task was completed. Greens Point, though, was still caught midstream in the biggest storm that had ever hit it, and the town has been whacked by storms flying up and down the Ohio River Valley. At that point in the case, nobody, including myself, could be sure of the eventual outcome.

✳ ✳ ✳

Despite the big hullabaloo surrounding my arrests of Lou and Duke, smaller activities, unnoticed by most, continued. After I met with Bob and Mayor Stubbs, the rest of the week wound down with tuning up my investigation for Bob's prosecution of Lou and Duke in court. The inventory process, basically tagging the evidence and signing the tags, was accomplished without incident. Outside of the investigation and prosecution, Norman was still lost upon the overgrown estate of Muriel Horner. He lived on the outskirts of town in his shack, without any future offered to him. The town government had nothing to offer him. Betsy pressed me to do something for him. Betsy especially pressed for those forgotten, Norman in particular.

Sunday afternoon shone like a southern spring should. The light blue sky was dotted with white puffs of clouds. A gentle breeze whisked up from the Ohio River Valley. In the breeze, the sweet fragrance of the valley wild flowers engulfed the outskirts of town.

I picked up Reverend Betts after lunch. We drove out in the squad car to the Horner estate. On the drive out to the farm, I baited the reverend for his thoughts on Norman. Reverend Betts played his hand close to the chest.

"Well now, Reverend, you and the church are the proud new owners of some of the choicest farmland around Greens Point. I'd say that it's time to till the land."

"I've been considering the same idea, Sam."

I drove on a bit and then cast off a thought. "You know, Norman knows the farm better than anybody. He's big and strong too—as strong as an ox. His muscle could help you out."

Reverend Betts remained silent.

"If he stayed on," I continued, "he'd be helping himself out too."

On that comment, the reverend just nodded. I couldn't do much more. I was up against the church.

We pulled up the stone drive and parked in front of the worn gray barn with Norman's attached shed. As we climbed out of the car, Norman walked out of the barn. In my opinion, he was better than any watchdog for the estate.

Norman walked over to the car and smiled. "Hello, Sheriff, Reverend."

"I told you we'd be back to talk to you, didn't I?"

"I remember, Sheriff Sam. You sure did."

"How have you been?" I asked.

"I'm doin' okay."

"How's the farm?" asked the reverend.

"All's the same. The cows are fed and milked. The chickens are droppin'. I hosed down the pigs yesterday."

We started drifting toward Norman's shed. I stopped halfway. "Why don't we go inside the house?"

"You're the sheriff," Norman said.

The three of us walked over to the back porch. Norman didn't open the door. The reverend appeared to be just along for the ride. So I turned the knob and stepped inside the house.

We stepped inside a time warp. Aside from the dust, the kitchen was set orderly with the ruffled dark-blue-and-white checkered curtains, the dark-blue place mats on the oak drop leaf table, and the plates inside the Hoosier cabinet up against the wall. Nothing was out of place.

I pulled out a thin oak spindle back chair from the drop leaf table and sat down. The reverend followed me and sat. Norman remained standing and leaned up against the sink. I noticed frozen clock hands above the white-and-black stove.

"This house looks well kept," said Reverend Betts.

"This could be one of the best farms around Greens Point," I said.

Norman smiled.

"Norman," began the reverend, "could you run the farm?"

I squinted and nodded at Norman, hoping the reverend didn't notice me.

Norman glanced at me and then back at the reverend. "Reverend, sir, I don't think so. I just tend to the chores, if you know what I mean."

Of course, the reverend didn't know what Norman meant. But I did. Norman could run the farm. He had been running it for years. He might not have been able to manage the books, but he knew how to feed and hose. I had to butt into the dialogue. "Norman, you've been tending to the cows and pigs for years. You've been running the farm."

Norman looked over at me. He grinned from ear to ear. He had a friend. Then he looked right back at the reverend. "I've been runnin' the farm for years. I milk the cows and feed the chickens. I know where each pig likes the hose."

Reverend Betts smiled. I wished I knew what the smile meant.

"Norman," I interrupted, "Mrs. Horner gave the farm to the reverend." Norman shot a look at me.

I pressed on rather boldly. "You raised the animals for Mrs. Horner, so you could raise them for the reverend, couldn't you?"

Norman again shot a look at me and then looked back at the reverend. "Sure I could. I raised them for Mrs. Horner."

I was now done. I had backed Norman for the reverend. Somebody had to do the thinking and talking for him. The big fellow had nobody to watch out for him. I, and especially Betsy, wanted Norman to stay on the farm. I picked up no hint of the reverend's position from his calm face.

"Would you like to stay on the farm, Norman?" asked Reverend Betts. Norman glanced at me.

I blinked and nodded hard back at Norman.

"I sure would, if I could. I got nowheres else to go."

With that, a smile spread out on Reverend Betts's face. Norman appeared to have scored what I had been trying to score for him.

Norman only half-smiled back at the reverend. The other half was caught by confusion.

About a half a minute passed without anybody saying anything. Norman's face seemed to say "What's next?" Reverend Betts stared into his clasped hands. I offered an empty smile to Norman.

"Well, Reverend," I began, "would you like to see anything else around the farm?"

The reverend raised up his eyes. "I don't think so, not now."

A thought struck me. "Why don't we walk back to Norman's shed?" Before the reverend had a chance to answer, I added, "It's by the squad car."

The reverend nodded. Norman was completely confused.

"Let's go," I said. I stood up, followed by the reverend and Norman. We walked over to the shed. Norman hesitated as we stopped in front of his door. I don't believe the reverend had ever really seen his shed.

"Let's go inside," I said.

Norman pushed open the wooden plank door, and we all walked inside. He stepped over, farthest from the door, by the wood-burning cast iron stove. I followed Norman, and the reverend followed me. I stepped over by his cot and spotted the Bible sitting on top of the pillow. I stepped aside. "Where's your harmonica?" I asked in good fun.

"Oh, that. I put it away under my pillow."

Reverend Betts glanced over at the pillow and saw the Bible. He stepped over to the bed and picked up the Bible. "Do you read the Bible, Norman?"

"I try."

"He reads the Bible every night," I followed up.

Reverend Betts rubbed the old worn black leather Bible in the palms of his hands. "It feels like you've put it to good use."

"It keeps me company."

I stepped farther out of line between the reverend and Norman.

"The Bible is company to all who read it," continued the reverend.

"When I'm lonely or when I'm sad, I read it too," said Norman. "It makes me feel better. I sometimes think there's more than workin' this farm," he continued. "But I'm not too smart. I don't know what's outside the farm anymore. So I read the Bible."

The reverend set the Bible back down on the pillow. He stepped to the door. "Norman?" asked the reverend.

"Yes, sir, Mr. Reverend?"

"You just keep doing what you're doing. Work. Read the Bible. The Bible can tell you more than I'll ever be able to tell you."

I reached over and squeezed Norman's shoulder. He smiled his biggest smile from ear to ear and beyond. As we stepped out of his shed, I turned toward him. "I'll stay in touch. If you need anything, you just ask me now, won't you?"

He nodded, still smiling. I suspected he had never had such attention. He just stood there empty handed in his tiny shed, probably wishing he could do or give more to the reverend and me.

I followed the reverend to the squad car. As we drove back to church, the car ride was quiet. I didn't want to upset anything Norman had said or done. I let the reverend think.

After I pulled up by the church to let the reverend off, the reverend looked at me. "That Norman, he's more than I had figured. He's never been in for a sermon, has he, Sam?"

"None that I recall."

CHAPTER 9

Of course, I knew he had never been in our church, not even for Mrs. Horner's service, although I had seen him off by the bushes behind the tiny gathering at Holy Hill.

"He may know more about the Bible than I do," said the reverend.

With that and a grin, he climbed out of the county car. I threw the car in reverse and then pulled away.

I did whatever I could for Norman. Betsy would be happy. Reverend Betts, though, still didn't commit to allowing Norman to stay on the farm. Perhaps he was still waiting on Bernie Cain to clear the probate case in court.

No matter when, where, or how a person dies, a lawyer makes a case out of it and takes it into court, civil or criminal. I swear that a lawyer can make a case out of anything. Bernie Cain had Muriel Horner's estate in court, and Bob Hunt was taking two charged grave robbers into court. Norman and Lou and Duke's lives were hanging in the scales.

Chapter 10

U NFORTUNATELY for Greens Point, the trial against Lou and Duke was at hand. There was more at stake than the testimony and exhibits. Jeb had left all kinds of messages for me. A reporter from the *National Enquirer* had called. After I called back the reporter, I knew the end was near. The *Enquirer*, the country's largest circulating newspaper, was going to run an article on the case in an upcoming issue. I felt I had to act as the town's spokesman to preserve the order and dignity of Greens Point.

If the case had still been in my hands, I would have been better able to control the direction of the media. But the case was out of investigation and into court. Bob and Tony were getting most of the coverage. Still, I was the star witness and would have my day in court.

Tony Pinelli, the Clermont County public defender, was appointed to represent Lou and Duke. Tony had assistant public defenders who performed most of the daily court appearances for his office, but the media exposure lured Tony to court.

The legal profession is funny that way. I'd bet my bottom dollar, although I'm no gambler, that there is a direct relationship between media coverage and supervisor involvement. If the press is interested in a case, it seems like the boss is interested in trying the case. If the press is not, the boss isn't either.

I believe that relationship is universal, at least in Clermont County. In Greens Point, Bob and Tony rarely got involved in the day-to-day run-of-the-mill trials. I can't recall when I'd seen either in court. Then again, I don't have much of a reason to appear in court.

In our county, a handful of judges ride the circuit. The judges drive around the county on specified days to different towns to hear the traffic tickets and minor offenses. The chief judge of Clermont County, Judge Flynn, acted more-or-less like the top administrator. When the grave poaching broke ink, however, he assumed an active role. He was to preside over the trial.

Tony appeared at the arraignment on behalf of Lou and Duke. Up to the trial, I had always felt that Tony was all right for a public defender. I mean our residents were law-abiding folk. For the most part, they just didn't commit crimes and had no tolerance for those who did. In fact, he was appointed the public defender by the chief judge just because of his laid-back approach to crime. No hard-charging reformer could hold any public office in our county. Since the county had to have a public defender, he appeared the least harmful. So he was appointed. Regardless of his appearance, I still didn't trust anybody who earned a living from the county trough defending criminals.

Not that looks matter, but he looked as much like a public defender as just about anybody could. He was short, dark, and thin. Even more, he wore a full beard and wire-rimmed glasses. On the other hand, he also looked like a handful of farmers down in our county, without the bib overalls.

Arraignment sent Greens Point in a flurry. John Day, my deputy assigned to the courthouse, was worried about his duties bringing the prisoners in court out of the courtroom holding cell. John was nervous from the crowd. He'd never seen a crowd in court. After the *Enquirer* caught wind of the case, reporters from papers out of Paducah, Springfield, St. Louis, and Chicago filled the front rows of the courtroom.

In light of John's bum foot, the unprecedented crowd, and the pressure from the news coverage, I decided to double in with John on the courtroom detail. I fielded the questions from the reporters to ensure a proper image of the sheriff's office.

After the pleas of not guilty entered by Tony on behalf of Lou and Duke, Judge Flynn continued the case for a month. The question of bail was irrelevant because they had no funds. They were charged with three counts of possession of stolen property, theft, and destruction of a tomb, one count for each grave. All of the crimes were misdemeanors, offenses punishable with a maximum jail sentence of less than a year.

I had wanted Bob to approve a felony charge with a jail sentence over a year. He said he couldn't make any felony stick. Theft of property with a value over one hundred fifty dollars was a felony, but he said he didn't have all of the stolen jewelry for court. I said he didn't need all of the jewelry to convict them of a felony in front of a Clermont County jury. Probably unbeknownst to Jerome Taylor, we had found out that either he was swindled or his friends hadn't his kind of money. The pocket watch was gold plated and was not worth anywhere near one hundred and fifty dollars.

A few days after the arraignment, Tony asked for a meeting with Bob and myself to discuss ending the case short of trial. The meeting between us didn't work out so well. The problem, put simply, was Lou. Nonetheless, I didn't get the impression that the attorneys were pushing very hard to settle the case. I held back on my opinion.

When we all fell into a stalemate, I brought Lou out of the cell into my office. He sat on a chair before my desk. Throughout the entire discussion, he wore a stiff smile on his lips. He must have thought he was in complete control.

"Lou," Tony continued, "I'm sure the sheriff and the prosecutor would go easy on you for a plea. I'm not exactly telling you to plea yet, but they say they have solid evidence against you."

He roared at us. "I'm going down no matter what. If I go down, this whole town's going down. Go ahead. Punish me with another month or two in the can. I've done worse. I'll eat better than I've had in years, and I won't be sleeping out in the rain, like I was when the sheriff first met me."

Tony, Bob, and I weren't in such an outgoing mood. We sat and took it all in.

"Sheriff, three graves were robbed under your protection of the public. The public may stand for one, but probably not two, and definitely not three."

I was shocked at the little man's ruthless vein. Despite his small size, he packed a mean streak, the likes of which I had never seen. He was rotten and bitter. Although he had no prior bad dealings with our town, he hated everything our peaceful town stood for.

"What about Duke?" I tried.

That question halted the conversation temporarily. I knew Lou had a soft spot in his heart, however small, for Duke. For years, Lou had looked out for that big fellow. Unfortunately, at this stage in the case, I think Lou felt that I sensed his weak-spot and responded in defense.

"What about Duke? You asked me, so I'll ask you. You talked to him. If we go down, he'll get off easier than me. What are you trying to pull here,

Sheriff? I was beginning to like you before you began to try to pull this shit off."

My stomach sank. I had tried playing my hand and lost.

The court calendar in our county is thin. We don't encounter too much crime. Besides, the people around the county prefer to work out their own problems before court action and, especially, attorneys' fees.

After arraignment, Judge Flynn set a month date for discovery. Discovery is the word for a process whereby both sides exchange information collected during their investigations. The defense had little to nothing to tender. The prosecution had only my reports and the proceeds and tools that I had collected. Bob had turned over my reports to Tony, and Tony had examined the watch, belt, shoes, and tools. The case was winding down fast.

In big cities like Chicago, I hear it can take over a year to try a felony case and three to five years to try a simple accident case. I find it funny trying to find out just exactly what big-city dwellers view as backwards.

Tony threw a wrench in the wringer. On that month check date, he filed a motion to suppress evidence based upon lack of probable cause for the arrests. As I understood the motion, there was no merit in it. I ought to know because I made the arrests. He must have just been covering himself in his representation of Lou and Duke. Taken in that light, I didn't care what he filed. We were friends, but we didn't talk too much.

The motion was filed, evidence presented in the testimony of myself, and arguments heard. Tony lost. Judge Flynn ruled that I had had probable cause to arrest them when I had seen the pocket watch at the general store, the mud-covered shovel and pick in the back of the truck, and the brown leather shoes and belt on Lou. I believe Tony knew I had probable cause but felt obligated to file the motion. I really can't fault the man for doing his job, especially with all that publicity.

Probable cause or not, common sense told me to stop those two fellows at that time. I operate on common sense, and if the law doesn't, then it should. Common sense generally proves right. As Betsy says, common sense is our rudder in life.

After a few more short continuances to make sure all was in order, Judge Flynn set the case down for jury selection. Jury selection is the most boring part of a jury trial. The lawyers bump off, or excuse, the people whom each doesn't want to sit on the jury. In Clermont County, jury selection isn't too important. All of the possible jurors are just about the same. Our county doesn't have a big blend of people. Most of the people are farmers, tradesmen, or small business owners. They pay their taxes and mortgages and follow the law. Odds were still in favor of conviction, regardless of which twelve finally sat in the jury box.

But guilt was not going to be the sole point of the trial. The way I was beginning to size up the situation, not only were Lou and Duke on trial, but Clermont County was too. Big-city reporters would be sitting in court, just waiting to report any blunder by any official from a small town like Greens Point.

For some reason, a lot of people in big cities poke fun at us who live out in the country or in small towns. We don't have symphonies or ballets, but we also don't have the daily murders and rapes. I felt this mishap at Holy Hill gave the nosy reporters a chance to belittle and embarrass what I believe to be the good, peaceful life. I felt we had to prove to the outsiders that, despite this mishap, Greens Point was still that friendly small town that ran day after day on the good works and wishes of families, neighbors, and friends.

The Monday set for jury selection was hot and humid. Greens Point is farther south than half of Kentucky. As a result, spring and summer rise up out of the gulf onto the southern tip of Illinois at least one to two months ahead of the northern half of the state. The crimes broke in spring, and after discovery status hearings, the case was continued to August. The main courtroom had two tall fans set at the rear corners to help our antiquated air conditioning, but Judge Flynn ordered John to shut them off during jury selection so the court reporter, attorneys, defendants, and he could hear the prospective jurors' answers.

The old courthouse is the prettiest building in town, except for our Baptist church. The courthouse and church look somewhat the same, but the tower clock rises higher than the cross on top of the steeple. The main courtroom on the second floor has a high, ornate ceiling and long rows of wooden benches for the public, like the pews in church. The center aisle floor is worn wood and creaks under foot. The judge's bench stands high and mighty, almost six feet above the floor. The chairs for the attorneys, witness, and jurors are wooden ladder-back chairs that screech when slid over the wood floor boards. The walls are partly covered by beadboard panels half a door high, with hand-carved trim. The thick wooden tables for the prosecution, facing the bench, and the defendants, facing the jury box, fill in the inner well of the courtroom, separated from the public benches by a wooden rail and swinging gates.

Judge Flynn fidgeted up on the bench. The prospective jurors sat cordially but uncomfortably on the public benches. The judge broke jury selection into two parts. During the first part, he asked the room full of prospective jurors general questions aimed at uncovering general biases and prejudices. After that screening, his procedure was to read out the names of twelve prospective jurors to sit in the jury box to answer more specific questions. Before he began this second part, lunchtime had arrived.

I walked over to Tucker's for lunch. All the tables were filled, as were the bar stools. From across the bar, Tucker shrugged his shoulders at me. For being such a regular customer, I expected more than a shrug from his shoulders.

The publicity of the trial had proved to be a real boon for local business. Tucker's was running full at lunch and dinner and especially after dinner, up and down the bar for drinks. Over at the general store, Clara was all smiles. After all, as she informed the out-of-towners, the criminals were arrested before her eyes, right at the very spot her customers were standing. At Miller's Garage, Tommy was servicing all kinds of cars. He would throw his thumb back over his shoulder and tell the visitors how he was given custody of the criminals' pickup truck parked alongside the gas station. I was proud of our town for the way they welcomed all of the visitors. Tucker, though, could have welcomed one less visitor for lunch and held a table or stool for me.

"Sheriff Carter?" called out a voice from a corner table.

I turned around and looked at a table full of out-of-towners.

"We have an extra chair here. Why don't you join us?"

I wasn't too fond of joining a table full of people I didn't know. At a second glance, they looked like reporters too. The gurgle in my stomach pulled me over to their table.

As I approached their table, they took writing pads and sport jackets off of the remaining chair. I knew I shouldn't have expected such an offer of Southern hospitality. Being the star witness, I figured these reporters wanted to pump me for a story.

"Sheriff, I'm Howie Schwartz, *Chicago Sun Times*. That's Russ Jacobs, *St. Louis Post-Dispatch*. Those two across the table are Tom Downs, Paducah, and Matt Best, from the state capital, Springfield."

"I'm glad to meet you all."

Howie was the oldest of the bunch. Russ and Tom looked the same, very unnoticeable. Matt was short and thin, and his neck arched forward from his shoulders to resemble a rooster.

After I took a seat, all of them tried to act relaxed, but I could tell they weren't. No matter how reporters look on the surface, something is always bubbling inside their heads. I've never had a reporter friend and can't say I would ever want one. A person can't relax with reporters around. They have quick eyes, too, that bounce all over the person hooked into their conversations. It seemed to me that I wasn't going to get a break that day, even during lunch. I wished I hadn't finished the ham last night.

"This is some crazy case, Sheriff," Howie opened up.

"Well now, Mr. Schwartz, I'm sure you've covered some crazy cases up there in Chicago."

"No, not really, mostly murders and rapes. Occasionally, we get a strange twist in the criminal trials, witchcraft—"

"Or thirty-three bodies," slipped in Matt.

"We do have our multiple murders in Chicago, but we have more people in the city too," Howie responded.

The reporters laughed. I figured they had their own kind of humor. I wasn't too fond of living off of people and their tragedies.

"We don't have the people or murders down here," I said.

"Down here, life seems pretty dull," Mr. Schwartz continued.

"Peaceful," I said.

The more I looked at that Schwartz fellow, the more he began to look like a weasel.

"How's your case against them, Sheriff?" asked Russ.

"It's not my case anymore. It's the prosecutor's."

Russ smiled and backed off.

"When are you testifying?" asked Tom.

"Bob hasn't told me yet."

Tom backed off.

"You've run unopposed for three or four terms, am I correct?" Matt began.

"Three. That's correct."

"This trial would make a nice swan song or, taking the opposite view, launch to a higher office, wouldn't it?"

"I suppose it could."

Matt didn't back off. "Is Mayor Stubbs running again?"

"You'd have to ask him."

Matt tried a different approach. "Have you been to Springfield, Sheriff?"

"I was there a few years back."

"How'd you like it?"

"I didn't like the traffic."

"Is that all? You sound like you would like it up there in the state capital."

"I like Springfield better than Chicago."

"Maybe I'll see you up there sometime in the future."

"Maybe."

Matt was the most dangerous of the bunch. He was the least direct and therefore the most lethal. If and when he took a shot, he fired undercover but shot to kill. Although he spoke with a Southern Illinois drawl, he was running on a political vein. I'm sure he had picked off more than one politician with his pen.

"May I take your orders?"

I looked up over my shoulder. "Janie, what are you doing waiting on tables?" Janie was married to Tucker.

"I'm helping him out during the trial."

"What's good here?" Howie asked Janie.

"Everything."

"Sheriff?" Matt asked.

"Tucker has a good grill. Burgers are big, but you might want to try that steak sandwich."

"How's the fish?" Russ asked.

"Fresh. With the Ohio down the road, the fried catfish can't be beat for miles around."

I doubt if Mr. Schwartz had ever tasted fried catfish. That was his loss. Too many people up north are put off by catfish. I don't know the reason. Maybe they taste too much like fish. Catfish are fried like any other fish.

I ordered the burger. Howie, Russ, and Tom ordered the steak sandwich. Matt ordered the catfish. I still didn't trust Matt. He had a beer. Howie and then Russ asked for a martini with some kind of foreign vodka. Tucker didn't carry that stuff. They had to settle for American vodka.

During our wait, the reporters tried to loosen me up with small talk about Greens Point. Howie had seen such small towns only on television. Tom seemed the best of the lot. Paducah isn't the biggest city, even by

Kentucky standards. Greens Point gets radar weather on television out of Paducah. Naturally, I felt a bond between us. I felt he understood me and the town best. I'm sure he'd been through a number of towns like Greens Point. Russ and Howie were looking at me and the town like a television comedy. Matt was looking for some political angle.

I can't fault people living in cities too much for not liking small towns. But I can hold against them their poking fun at our simple ways of doing things. First of all, I hear city dwellers are supposed to have open minds. I think they're supposed to have open minds because of all that's going on around them in the big cities. All that's happening is supposed to keep them from falling into a narrow rut. But the way I see them, they fall into so deep a rut that they can't see out of it to appreciate other ways of living.

Second of all, I don't see anything wrong with simple ways. Life is too big and short to be wasting time sidetracking and circling around direct paths to solutions to problems. In big cities, people are paid to sit around instead of solving problems. In fact, they sit around thinking up problems and making problems bigger to justify their jobs and pay. Instead of outright solving problems, they make up systems to solve problems. On top of that, they assign a person or group of people to analyze the systems they make up. Not stopping there, to complete the organization, they appoint another person or group of people to review the analysis reports, another to approve the reviewing reports, and still another to change the system.

It seems to me that they've dreamed up an organization so removed from the problem that they can no longer see the problem clearly. By the time the organization is built up, the problem has changed by lapse of time, the organization itself, or otherwise. This means that new studies and reports are begun and passed up the organization. I think big cities are built on top of this spinning around and around simple and direct solutions: the more spinning, the more paychecks. If the spinning ever stopped, the cities would grind to a halt.

For instance, up in Chicago, that Gacy fellow stood trial for killing thirty-three boys and young men and burying most of them under his house in a crawl space. Instead of trying him right off in Chicago, the lawyers and judge got together and decided to transfer the case farther north to Winnebago County for jury selection only. Then the chosen jurors boarded a bus and headed for Chicago for an extended stay.

The way I understand one of the main arguments for transfer was that the defense thought Gacy couldn't get a fair trial in Chicago on account of all that newspaper and television coverage of the crimes before the trial. Since the defendant had a right to file a motion to change the location of the trial, those defense attorneys were going to use it. And they did, right or wrong.

The attorneys took their client up away from Chicago and dropped him plunk down on our state's northern border in the middle of a blue-collar county, Winnebago County. Those workers hadn't seen all of the newspaper and television stories as the Chicagoans had. But that didn't matter one iota. Winnebago County didn't care about the news stories, and they certainly didn't care about any insanity defense. By exercising that right, the defense attorneys took Gacy away from the crazy city life and soft jurors to a solid county with regular jurors.

Those defense attorneys thought too hard and too much. They got mixed up in the law. They forgot that they didn't have to use a right just because it was in the law books. They lost sight of the solution to the problem: avoid a conviction for Gacy. By spinning around and around, they missed the mark, and Gacy got sentenced to death.

Right from the very start, they could have gotten their client the same by staying in Chicago and forgetting about all that legal fussing around.

Gacy's attorneys should have agreed to select the jury right there in Chicago. If a juror's going to be soft enough to go for some kind of insanity defense, that juror is going to be from Chicago, not Winnebago County. There's nothing difficult about that decision, if a person keeps thinking in simple terms.

In Clermont County, neither the jury selection nor the trial was going anywhere. There was a lot of news stories on the crimes, and there was a right to file a motion to transfer the case. But there was no reason to transfer the case. Transfer wasn't going to do a bit of good for Lou and Duke. The residents of the counties in Southern Illinois all look and think the same. They're tradesmen and farmers or small business operators living off of tradesmen and farmers.

The only exception might be Jackson County, where Southern Illinois University is and all those students and professors are. But there was no way Tony would be able to select Jackson County with Bob and Judge Flynn also taking part in the decision. Likewise, with the charges being no greater than misdemeanors, there was no way Tony could ever get a transfer up north to Chicago or another university town. For supposedly being simple and closed minded, Clermont County sure seems to see both sides of a problem.

After lunch, everybody assembled once again in the courthouse. The afternoon brought on the heat. With the fans off, most of the prospective jurors took to fanning themselves, a good number of them with paper napkins imprinted with Tucker's Bar and Grill. John turned the fans back on during recesses and breaks, but the press and public took the longer recesses and breaks out on the courthouse steps or under the old oaks standing in front of the courthouse.

During the afternoon, Judge Flynn resumed with part two of jury selection. By dinnertime, the jurors and alternates had been selected.

I'd like to say a few words about the jury. The makeup of the jury was roughly half men and half women. In Clermont County, that split doesn't necessarily mean anything. In our county, women were equal to men long before the equality uproar hit the cities around the country. Men and women on the farms worked equally hard. Both husband and wife pitched in to pay off the mortgage on the farm.

Helen Barnes was an example. Helen was selected for the jury. She was a big-boned woman with a hearty, husky air about her. I've seen her again and again clipping down the county roads in her pickup truck, with a couple of young calves in the truck bed. Once in front of the barn, she runs them into a pen to get them used to the farm and drinking milk from a pail.

Calves don't know how to drink milk from a pail right after they're taken from their mother. I suppose people unfamiliar with country life wouldn't know such a simple fact. A farmer has to teach a baby calf how to drink milk from a pail. Helen would dunk her finger in the milk and then jam her finger in the calf's mouth like an udder. Then she would lead the calf's head with her finger to the milk pail.

Although most people drink milk at least once a day, they don't know such simple facts on how they get that milk they drink. The same goes for the food they eat. I figure most city people don't know how many ears of corn grow on a stalk. Some guess two, some six. Others guess all the way up to twelve. They must eat corn at least once a month and don't know how it grows. I find funny what people nowadays consider intelligence.

Getting back to the jury, in contrast to Helen, Zachary Horton—old Slim—was also sitting on the jury. Slim was retired but used to be the bookkeeper for the last barge company in town. He was just five feet tall and all skin and bones. He wore eyeglasses with a wire rim and thick lenses and had those callused elbows from leaning on a desktop all day. With one breath, Helen could blow Slim over.

I couldn't see Helen favoring a defendant more than Slim. Both have worked hard over the years just to pay off their debts and bills. People in our county don't work to be able to buy a vacation home or cushion their retirement. Neither Helen; Slim; Carl Hooks, the butcher; nor Eunice James, the druggist's sister-in-law, should have had any special pity for a couple of drifters bent on grave poaching.

Any possibilities for Lou and Duke would have had to be a juror like Ester DuPrey. Ester was a school teacher in the local grammar school. She was only a few years out of college. The DuPreys had lived in or about Greens Point for generations. Despite her firm family foundation, her recent release from college and single status possibly opened her mind to consider any new idea, however small. She was short and frail, and her hair was wiry but thin. Her smile lit the lenses on her eyeglasses. She loved reading. Tony grinned. Bob was too busy studying his notes to hear her answer.

Denny Simpson might also have proved to wander. The Simpsons had been vegetable farmers for decades in Clermont County. Their days revolved around hard work, little sleep, and little pay. Regardless, Denny's parents recouped their efforts they expended from the weekly sermons every Sunday.

Denny, however, represented that young man with one foot still back on the farm and the other venturing into new ground, generally the city sidewalks. He was a strapping young man with a broad back and shoulders. Although he didn't stay on the high school wrestling team, he was part of the backbone of the team before he quit. Bob grinned at the former high school athlete. Tony quickly jotted down the sport in his notes.

While just butting into manhood, the young powerful body was poking almost blindly about into new ground, beyond the tilled soil of his parents' farm. He was energetic and restless, trying job after job. He hadn't held one job for over six months. His parents didn't understand him, but they understood enough to let him try, at least for a short while longer.

The jury was selected in one day. Judge Flynn was determined to wrap the trial up in a week.

The courtroom was packed. All was set, but too set, I was afraid. Something was bound to explode.

Chapter 11

HOSPITALITY is a Southern calling card. Judge Flynn was born and raised in Clermont County. He set out the welcome mat for the press from around the country. He ordered that the front row of benches on either side of the center aisle be reserved for the press—especially the television artists, who merited an unrestrained view of the principals during the trial. In good turn, an artist from a Chicago television station showed appreciation by offering a color sketch of him during jury selection. The artist suggested that he frame and hang the sketch in his chambers like the judges in Chicago. He did.

I told John that I would help him during the trial. After all, he had that bum foot. Accordingly, I assigned him mainly to escort the jurors in and out of court and tend to their needs. Being the main witness for the prosecution, I couldn't get too close to them. Consequently, I led Lou and Duke in and out of the courtroom and sat behind them in the courtroom during the trial—for security reasons, of course. From this viewpoint, I could watch the entire trial firsthand. Later, I gave Betsy a sketch in color of Lou, Duke, and me sitting in the courtroom. I had the sketch framed and hung in our parlor.

The trial unveiled one of the biggest crimes ever in the history of Greens Point, Clermont County, and Illinois. In some ways, the trial of Lou and Duke surpassed the trial of Gacy. Our trial surpassed that trial and all of the other serial killer cases around the country in the sole character of the crime. No serial grave poacher had ever come to light in the press. For serial killers, there were Berkowitz, Bundy, and Gacy, but for serial grave poachers, only Lou and Duke. Small Greens Point, probably never heard of outside of Clermont County before the trial, was the site of the only serial grave poaching. For that reason, I felt all eyes around the country turned to Greens Point. Our town was destined for the history books. Without ever dreaming of a place in history, I found myself thrown into a major role in a historical event.

I'd be the first to admit that I never planned to plot a place in history. History doesn't allow such personal plans. History is borne out of the past. Only luck and timing can push one to the foreground of history. My investigation and capture of the culprits vaulted me into history. I fear I'm not overstating my place in history.

The rest of the principal actors in this event, for the most part, were good solid men. Bob Hunt represented the people of Clermont County. I can't say he was brilliant or even smart, but during trial, he worked harder than a farmer in a harvest sunset. He had no flare or charm, but he kept chugging hard and steady. His blunt forehead and thinning blond hair just captured this honest but unlucky fellow. Despite any of his shortcomings, Bob had that plain, blunt gumption of the old riverboat captains. Simply put, he was thick headed and stubborn, but he knew the basic ins and outs of trials the way the boat captains knew the main currents and bars along the Ohio and Mississippi down to the delta.

Bob can be faulted now and then for this and that, mostly small potatoes, but he carried his own load. I heard four prosecutors were assigned to the Gacy trial. That's one short of a basketball squad. Bob tried Lou and Duke alone.

Tony Pinelli, the public defender, was as fluent as Bob Hunt was mechanical. Bob knew the basic law and executed the fundamental trial skills, whereas Tony slipped and slid around those skills. I wasn't critical of either attorney. The two lawyers involved in the trial had opposite styles. Perched behind Lou and Duke, I had a keen view of the whole trial.

Judge Flynn would try to remain impartial during the trial, especially with all eyes of the press on him. He was competent, fair, and experienced. His knowledge of the law came from his experience, not the books.

He looked like a judge too. He had white hair that shone against the black robe. I noticed that he had his robe zipped down in front a couple of inches. I found funny the way his new blue shirts lit up his blue eyes.

I could never accuse Bob of falling prey to pretense. He was too dense and mechanical. Besides, his wife dressed him. In truth, I believe Bob probably felt uncomfortable in front of the press. He was scared of tripping on his feet. I'm not saying he was incompetent. He wasn't. He stepped slowly but very surely. He just didn't want to be hounded for his deliberate manner. The media coverage appeared to wear him down.

The press appeared to perk up Tony. He couldn't stand too tall, though, because first, he was barely five and a half feet tall, and second, the prosecution's case stacked up mightily against him. Still, I expected a few pops from Tony. The reporters and, through them, the legal community were watching him, and he couldn't stay in the public defender's office for his entire career.

I knew Lou was fired up to amuse the media. He had nothing left to lose. A man with nothing to lose is dangerous. He was a mean little man. He sat on the witness stand wrapped and curled like a rattler poised to lash out his answers.

In contrast, I felt some sympathy for Duke. He wasn't used to attention, let alone media from cities like Chicago, Springfield, St. Louis, and Paducah. His testimony would sound blunt and blank. He wouldn't know what words to use, for fear of upsetting Lou.

I can definitely say that he was unaware of the total picture. Maybe he knew he was being tried for doing wrong. But he certainly didn't know what the town and media were doing to him.

To me, the trial would only repeat my investigation and arrests before the jury. I would be the second witness, but I would testify the longest. I would be called to the stand to set the general framework for the case and set out for the jury step-by-step the discovery of the crimes and the investigation that led to the arrests of Lou and Duke; the recovery of the tools, pocket watch, shoes, and belt; and the statements. Bob would call a few other witnesses, just to tie up a few loose ends. I figured the guts of the trial would be the testimony of me against Lou and Duke, if they took the stand.

A trial generally begins with opening statements given by the attorneys for both sides. In opening statements, attorneys are supposed to tell the jurors what each side expects the evidence will show during the trial. Opening statements are not to be considered as evidence.

"Are the attorneys ready for opening statements?" Judge Flynn called out from the bench.

Bob gave a quick nod.

"Defense is ready, Your Honor," answered Tony.

Tony had already begun to outshine Bob.

"State, you may proceed."

Bob walked stiffly over before the jury box. He appeared hesitant and slightly confused at the start, like a bull turned loose in a new pen.

"Judge Flynn, Mr. Pinelli, ladies and gentlemen of the jury," he began. "If death be sad, then let it be. The death of a loved one fills family and friends with grief. Through the visitation and funeral, the living offer their final farewell to the departed. This departure is made less painful through the hope of eternal peace. Grave robbery—"

"Objection," Tony hollered out. "The prosecutor's comments are far beyond the limits of opening statement."

The slow but steady Bob turned and looked at Tony and then the judge. Judge Flynn appeared to be enjoying Bob's speech. Nevertheless, he called out to Bob.

"Mr. Hunt, are you going to start telling the jurors what you expect the evidence is going to show?"

"Yes, Judge."

"Then get on with it."

"Your Honor, may I have a ruling on my objection?" Tony asked.

"Oh, yes. Objection is sustained."

Tony was setting the ground rules—his rules—right off the bat.

"Just this past April, one rainy Friday night," continued Bob, "Sheriff Sam Carter drove the squad car homeward."

Following proper courtroom decorum, I kept my stare on Bob, although I felt a few jurors glance my way.

"On the sheriff's way home, he had to pass Bender's Creek over the thin old bridge. The only light on the road fell from the headlight beams on the county car. As the sheriff's car bumped onto the old wooden bridge, the headlights flashed on a pickup truck on the other side of the creek. Now, Sheriff Carter, being a lawman sworn to uphold the law in all respects—"

"Objection."

Again, Judge Flynn was caught enjoying Bob's speech. After he had collected himself and reflected on the objection, he again instructed Bob.

"Mr. Hunt, you are entitled to discuss your expectation of the evidence only."

"Judge, I was."

Judge Flynn's eyebrows arched up like an owl. "Be that as it may, proceed with your expectation of the evidence."

Judge Flynn glanced over at Tony. "Sustained."

To me, my duty to uphold the law was a fact, plain and simple. I thought Bob was doing fine and Tony up to no good.

I caught a glimpse of that reporter from Chicago—the one that looked like a weasel wearing a mustache. He winked a half smile over to me. I didn't exactly know what his wink meant. He could have been backing me up, but then again he could have been taking a poke at me. I expected the latter. Those freewheeling reporter types always gripe against law and order. They like to tear down to make news. I just looked ahead at Bob.

"Continuing where I left off, Sheriff Carter parked the squad car in front of the truck. As he walked past the truck bed, he noticed a shovel and a pick stuck with mud. Although he figured the truck might have gotten stuck, he found all tires free and clear. Sheriff Carter did find footprints and broken branches leading down underneath the bridge. He walked down and under the bridge."

Bob paused and pushed back his thin hair. He began again but loosened up. "'Howdy,' called out the short, thin stranger," Bob said. "The tall, huge stranger remained silent throughout most of the discussion but for his repetition of his short partner's words. No, the strangers weren't stuck. They said they were taking cover from the rain and eating dinner, too, from the sheriff's sight of an empty can of beans by the strangers. Yes, they knew Greens Point was nearby. They said they weren't fond of towns. Mud stuck on their pants."

Bob checked his notes in front of him on the lectern and then moved on. "After getting reassurances they would be on their way in the morning, Sheriff Carter left. Two weeks later, he was to recall the muddy tools. The invasion of three graves was to pull those memories into his mind during his investigation. The strangers' faces were to rise again. Inside of Jeffries General Store, Sheriff Carter arrested those strangers for robbing three graves."

After plodding so painfully slow through his opening statement, Bob paused at the end and concluded, "Ladies and gentlemen, those strangers now sit across from you as the defendants in this case." He turned slowly and pointed over toward Lou and Duke.

Throughout Bob's statement, he spoke slowly and deliberately. But for the finger-pointing at the end, he struck no poses and cast no gestures, except maybe the time he patted down his hair, if that can be called a gesture. Since I'm not a lawyer, I couldn't tell. I suspected it wasn't.

He talked for about thirty minutes. He covered my basic investigation through Haney's discoveries at Holy Hill; my arrests of Lou and Duke at

Jeffries General Store; my recovery of the pocket watch, belt, shoes, and tools; and Lou and Duke's confessions to me.

The word *confessions* set off an outburst from Tony. He hollered out an objection and jumped out of his chair. He demanded the confessions be called statements, according to the Illinois Pattern Jury Instructions that were to be given to the jury at the end of the trial for the jury's deliberation. Judge Flynn agreed. From his objections, I began to see Tony's defense even before his opening statement.

In contrast to Bob during his opening statement, Tony moved a whole lot more but said a whole lot less. Tony talked no more than fifteen minutes. He barely mentioned my investigation.

"A joker and a dreamer. That's what Lou and Duke are. You'll hear Duke on the witness stand. He has little, if any, mind of his own. If he doesn't have anybody to tell him what to say or do, he says or does nothing. You heard the prosecutor say that, under Bender Creek Bridge, Duke only repeated Lou's words. You'll also learn that the statement the sheriff claims he took from Duke is nothing but a dream."

I didn't care for that crack, even if it was just law talk. I felt Tony's pointed finger aimed at me was cheap. That weasel-faced reporter winked at me again.

Tony paced back and forth and pointed here, there, and everywhere. "Lou's nothing but a smart mouth. Remember, he has nothing to lose, no money, no job, no home. He's having the time of his life on stage here in Greens Point. He has the whole town and maybe the entire country chasing the biggest whopper of a joke he's ever told. He'll tell you all about the whopper when he testifies. No matter how bad you may find his sense of humor, I'll remind you right now that a joke is no crime."

Tony continued pacing and pointing. "Finally, two muddy tools seen on a rainy night aren't much of any kind of evidence. Two dry tools seen out in a rainy night might mean something, but muddy tools on a rainy night mean nothing. I'm waiting to see if the state tries to introduce mud samples to close in on the culprits."

I was never fond of ridicule disguised as humor. There's a place and time for poking fun and making sport of people. Church and court aren't the places or times.

***

I wasn't called as the first witness because, as Bob explained to me, he wanted to start off with a greater sense of alarm. I didn't think Clermont County jurors needed theatrics. Then again, I wasn't the prosecutor. Instead of me, the prosecution called Haney.

What I'm about to say now isn't intentionally unkind to Haney, but he looked like hell. His oily hair was a mess, his eyes glassy, and the knot on his necktie askew. He didn't answer one question without mumbling or rambling. If the decision had been mine, I would have begun with a firmer step.

"Mr. Haney, do you need a glass of water?" asked Bob, not a minute after he began his direct examination.

"No, I'm all right."

Sure, he was all right. Bob had him sitting straight up with a few shots of vodka.

"Would you tell the jurors what you did that Friday afternoon?"

"Like I started to say, I was making my rounds. Beginning in spring, at the end of the week, I drive around Holy Hill just to check out the grounds."

"What was the weather like?"

"It was raining on and off the entire day."

"Did you see anything unusual?"

"It was awful."

"Objection, Your Honor, an unresponsive, bald conclusion," Tony snapped.

"Just the facts, Haney," Judge Flynn cautioned. "Sustained," the judge added.

"May I have a glass of water, Judge?"

"Deputy, if you would."

I gave John a nod of the head to fetch Haney a glass of water.

Haney plugged along slowly. He didn't look once at the jurors.

"What a bang of a start, Bob," I thought.

Well, after bumbling around for five minutes, Bob finally led Haney to the Albrecht grave. "Did you walk over to the pile of dirt?"

"Sure, I walked over there."

"Did you look over the pile?"

"Sure."

"Tell the jurors what you saw."

"Objection, leading," Tony called out. He cut into the roll Bob was beginning with Haney.

"What did you see?" Judge Flynn asked, rephrasing the question. So much for Tony's tactic.

"I saw a coffin."

"Where was the coffin you saw?" Bob asked.

"I saw the coffin in the grave dug on the other side of the dirt pile."

"What was the condition of the coffin?"

"The top was split off."

"Did you look inside?"

"No."

"What did you do?"

"I raced back to the office and called Sheriff Carter."

After another five minutes, Bob finally led Haney back to the grave. I knew I had to practically drag him back to the grave after the sun had set. Luckily for Haney, Bob spared the jurors those details. I didn't get Haney's call until suppertime. I suppose lawyers don't consider details too important.

"Where did the sheriff point the flashlight?"

"He aimed it into the grave."

"What did you see?"

Haney took a deep gulp of water. "I only saw the face."

I didn't recall Haney being that close to the grave. I suppose that was just another detail.

"What did the face look like?"

"Objection, Your Honor, irrelevant and prejudicial," Tony called out.

"Overruled."

"May I have a sidebar?" asked Tony.

Judge Flynn stood and walked to the side of the courtroom opposite the jury box behind Lou and Duke. The attorneys and court reporter followed him and stood before him with their backs to the jurors.

Although I wasn't particularly on top of all the legal terms being tossed about during the sidebar conference, Tony sounded good. He knew his law business. Since I was seated behind Lou and Duke, I could overhear their arguments. I guess Tony had asked for this conference so the jurors couldn't overhear the arguments.

To make long legal arguments short, if possible, Tony didn't want the jurors to hear a description of the faces because the descriptions would inflame the jurors' passions against the defendants with facts irrelevant to the elements of the charged crimes. He especially didn't want the jurors to see the photographs of the open coffins that I took and he saw, under the discovery rules before trial. In addition to prejudice, he objected to the photographs because I had taken them in the daylight on the next day.

Bob wanted the witness to identify the photographs and describe the corpses to prove circumstantially that the coffins were opened and the jewelry was taken from the corpses inside the coffins. Judge Flynn thought a description would actually be less frightening than the runaway imagination of the jurors. The judge also let Haney identify all of the photographs if he was able to recognize what they depicted, so long as he noted any change in circumstances from what they depicted and what he saw. Heck, I figured that, since the defendants had opened the coffins, they couldn't try to keep them closed to the jurors.

Judge Flynn climbed back onto the bench. "Overruled."

"Do you remember the question?" Bob continued.

"Yes, I do," Haney answered. "I could only see a blur of bone and black holes for eyes."

Bob walked up to Haney.

"I'm handing you Exhibit Number 6A out of People's Group Exhibit 6," continued Bob. "Can you tell the jurors what it is?"

Haney glanced at the photograph and then looked away. "That's a photograph of the open coffin."

"Does that photograph truly and accurately depict the manner in which the open coffin looked to you?"

"Yes, except the photograph shows the coffin during the day."

Eventually, Bob led Haney through the other two graves while handing him two photographs for each grave. The testimony was so choppy that I grew bored within ten minutes. Bob needed a witness to deliver concrete facts in an orderly way. Luckily for him, I was to do the heavy lifting with the photographs of the corpses.

During cross-examination, Tony made mincemeat out of Haney. Tony stood right in front of Haney as he pursued his line of questioning. "You never saw anybody digging up those graves, did you?"

"No."

"You never saw anybody in the cemetery who didn't belong there, did you?"

"No."

Tony walked over by Lou and Duke. "You never saw my two clients, sitting here in court, in your cemetery at any time, did you?"

"No."

"Pardon me. I didn't hear your answer."

He sure did.

"No, I didn't see them."

Tony walked over from standing near Lou and Duke back by the witness stand. "Who does the grave digging for you?"

"Norman Tibbs."

"He's a big man, right?"

"I'd say so."

"He could probably lift a loaded coffin by himself, couldn't he?"

"Probably."

Haney slipped out his answer before Bob could choke out his objection. Tony walked back to the lectern. "You don't pay him much, do you?"

"Objection, Judge," Bob called from his seat. "Relevancy."

"I'll withdraw that question," Tony quickly shot back.

"Mr. Haney, do you know where Norman lives?"

"I do."

"He lives in an old chicken coop attached to a barn, doesn't he?"

"Objection."

"Fine, Mr. Hunt," Tony responded.

"He lives in a shack on the Horner farm," Haney blurted out.

"He lives in a tiny shack?"

"It's small."

Judge Flynn let the examination go. Bob wasn't quick enough to slip objections between the questions and answers.

Tony bounced to another topic. "You keep records for each grave, am I right?"

"Right."

"The records have names and dates, right?"

"Right."

"But the records have no lists of property, right?"

"Right."

"So there is no record listing jewelry or clothing on the bodies in the coffins, isn't that right?"

"That's right."

Tony then slipped in a curve that even I hadn't expected. "Regarding records and property, Mr. Haney," Tony began, "you have Holy Hill insured, don't you?"

"Definitely."

"Damage to the grounds, let's say graves, should be a recoverable loss, shouldn't it?"

"Yes."

I looked over at Bob. His forehead was furrowed.

"Three recoverable claims could surely boost your business income, couldn't they?"

"Objection, Judge," Bob called out. "Mr. Haney isn't on trial here. The defendants are."

"Business ain't that bad," mumbled Haney.

"You wouldn't turn away from a windfall from your insurance though, would you?" Tony asked Haney.

"Judge," called out Bob, "I ask that you put an end to this line of questioning."

"But for this trumped-up trial against these two men, nobody in town would have found out about your insurance proceeds?"

"Judge," begged Bob.

"I have no further questions, Your Honor."

Tony walked slowly back to his chair.

"Judge, I move to strike the last line of questions from the record and ask you to instruct the jury to disregard them," Bob asked.

"Let the record stand for what it's worth," answered Judge Flynn.

Tony was beginning to make a case for himself. Luckily for Bob, I was up next on the witness stand.

Chapter 12

J UDGE Flynn broke for lunch. I didn't enjoy mine. Bob kept me in his office cornered by a cold beef sandwich with no ketchup. He knew I liked ketchup.

He didn't even give me a chance to enjoy the sandwich. He kept bombarding me with questions—questions he had already asked me ten times. Not content with all of those questions, he kept suggesting answers for me. I couldn't imagine his gall. His prosecution rode on my shoulders. I broke the crimes, made the arrests, and recovered the evidence. Now, he was pretending to control me.

If I had been allowed to talk to the jurors the way I wanted, my testimony would have been smoother and more convincing. I could have handled Tony. But Bob wouldn't let me. He didn't even compliment my uniform, which Betsy had washed and pressed with the iron, and my badge, which I had polished.

One of the biggest problems with lawyers is their blindness. They can't see anything beyond their law books, law talk, and law. They think the only right way is their way. Too often, they forget that witnesses, and especially the jurors, aren't lawyers.

After a couple of minutes with introductory background information, Bob focused his direct examination of me on my first meeting with Lou and Duke under Bender Creek Bridge. To avoid repetition of testimony about the discovery of the graves, I'll plunge ahead to my arrests of Lou and Duke.

"After lunch, Sheriff," continued Bob, "what did you do?"

"After that meat loaf sandwich with ketchup Betsy had made for me," I began. I figured Bob needed help. He wasn't as quick or clever as Tony. So, by reciting details, my credibility before the jurors would be enhanced.

I had picked up this practice over my many years of experience and the summer issue of one of Hank's police magazines.

"I walked down Main Street," I continued. "Then I spotted that pickup truck I had seen a couple weeks before by the bridge over Bender's Creek. The truck was parked in front of Jeffries General Store. As I walked closer, I saw the shovel and pick still covered with mud in the truck bed. Then I saw somebody behind the driver's wheel. I stepped up to the window on the driver's side."

"Objection to the narrative, Your Honor."

"Sustained."

Tony knew how to break a man's stride.

"What happened next?"

"I saw that the driver was Lou. As we greeted each other and I determined Lou and Duke were just passing through Greens Point, I detected Lou was playing close to the chest."

"Objection to the sheriff's conclusion. I move to strike his answer."

"Sustained. Sheriff Carter, try to testify to only what you saw, heard, and did. His answer as to what he detected will be stricken."

I nodded to the judge but was growing impatient with Tony for the interruptions.

"Realizing Duke was left alone in the store, I slipped off into the general store."

"Did you see anybody in the store?"

"I did."

"Who did you see?"

"Clara Jeffries and Duke."

"Pardon me for a moment, Sheriff, but do you see Lou and Duke, you just mentioned, in this courtroom today?"

"I do."

"Would you mind pointing them out, please?"

"Of course not." I pointed.

Bob noted my identification of Lou and Duke in court for the record taken down by the court reporter.

"Where was Mrs. Jeffries?"

"Clara, with her hair pinned up as she always does, was behind the counter by the cash register."

"What did you do next?"

"I stepped next to Duke and asked him for his reason for stopping in the general store."

"Did he answer?"

"Yes, he said he was buying cigarettes for Lou and gum balls for himself."

I described the manner in which Duke had fumbled in his pockets for change, Lou had blasted the horn on the truck, and Duke had fumbled faster. "He slapped a pocket full of change on the countertop, together with a gold pocket watch," I told the jury. I explained to the jury how I had reached for the watch before Duke could grab the pile and pull it back into his pocket. "Upon a spot interrogation of Duke, I learned only that Lou found the watch and gave it to Duke," I answered.

At this point in my testimony, Bob approached me on the witness stand. "Handing you People's Exhibit Number 1, can you identify it?" Bob asked.

"I can."

"What is it?"

"This is the pocket watch I took from Duke."

"How do you know this is the same watch?"

"This pocket watch has the same J. T. engraving that was on the pocket watch I took from Duke."

"How did Duke look when you took the watch?"

"Confused, no frightened."

"Objection."

"Sustained."

"Your Honor, would you please order the jurors to disregard the prosecutor's question and the sheriff's answer?"

"I will."

He did. But the damage was done.

Later in my testimony, Bob had me describe the way I had obtained the tools, clothes, and statements. He had me identify the tools and clothes.

After Bob sat down, Tony sprang up. "May I cross, Your Honor?"

Judge Flynn winked at the jurors and limped off the bench. Bob and Tony followed him into his chambers. John led the jurors out of the courtroom to the jury room. I was left sitting on the stand facing Lou and Duke and a crowded courtroom. The reporters and public began to stand to stretch their legs.

I sat ten minutes on the stand. My surprise fumed into anger. I sus-pected Judge Flynn had called the recess so he, the lawyers, the jurors, and the press could go to the restrooms. By the time the court was called back into session, I'm sure my face was crimson, right in time for Tony's cross-examination.

Tony walked straight at me. "I'm handing you Defense Exhibit Num-ber 1. You recognize it, don't you?"

"I do."

"You gave it to Duke, am I right?"

"Yes."

"You pulled it out of your official lost and found box, right?"

"Right."

"It ticked, but it didn't keep time, right?"

"Right."

Tony walked back to the lectern, holding the wristwatch out for the jurors to see. That Tony wouldn't let me answer but a word or two.

"You gave this watch, Defense Exhibit Number 1, to Duke after you took the pocket watch from him?"

"Yes, so?"

"So Duke could fall asleep listening to it tick, right?"

"He liked to listen to a watch tick at night."

"To fall asleep?"

"Objection," Bob called out.

"If the witness knows, he may answer," responded Judge Flynn.

"That's what Duke told me," I said.

Tony walked up to me again. "He told you he listened to the ticks at night to sleep?"

"I suppose so."

"He did?"

"Yes, he did."

"You gave Duke that broken watch because you felt sorry for the big simple fellow, didn't you?"

"Objection," Bob called out again.

"Sustained."

Tony paused. I wondered why Tony described Duke like that. I was starting to feel sorry for Duke, sitting across the jury with a blank stare. Then Tony walked back to the lectern and continued his examination. "Sheriff, did the pocket watch work?" he asked.

"No, it didn't tell time," I answered.

"Maybe I didn't make myself clear. I'll rephrase my question. Did the pocket watch tick?"

"No, it didn't tick."

"But Duke told you he listened for the pocket watch to tick to fall asleep, is that what you're telling this jury?"

Tony looked at the jury and back at me.

I had wondered how Duke could have fallen asleep listening to the ticks of a pocket watch that didn't tick. Being on the witness stand, I didn't have time for reflection. "That's what he told me."

Tony paused, shook his head, and moved to another topic. "When you first met Lou and Duke by Bender's Creek, Lou did all the talking, didn't he?"

"I suppose he did, most of it."

"What little Duke said, he repeated Lou?"

"Sort of."

"By 'sort of,' do you mean not word for word or not all of the time?"

"I guess both."

"So he did repeat Lou?"

"I suppose so."

"Yes?"

"Yes."

I was wondering where Tony would go next. Before he asked his next question, he positioned himself right in front of the jury. "Sheriff Carter, about Duke's so-called statement you claim you obtained from him, he said he thought the digging was a dream, didn't he?"

"He might have."

"Did he, or didn't he?"

"He did."

"Are you now telling these jurors that you and Duke sat in your office for a couple of hours talking about a dream?" Tony glanced at the jurors.

"We didn't talk a couple of hours," I answered.

"Well then, how about an hour?"

"Not even one hour."

"Well?" Tony asked me.

"Mr. Pinelli?" I asked him.

"You are telling these jurors you two sat for some period of time talking about his dream, aren't you?"

"I didn't believe him."

Tony paused a moment and walked up to me. "Your Honor, I ask that the sheriff's answer be stricken and he be instructed to answer the question I'm asking him."

"The answer is stricken. Mr. Pinelli, just ask him the question again."

"Sheriff, I'm not asking you whether or not you believed my client. That decision is for the jurors. The jurors have the duty to decide who's telling the truth around here, not you. Once again, you and Duke talked about his dream, didn't you?"

"Yes, he said he thought he was dreaming about the digging."

Tony walked slowly back to the lectern. "And all the while you two talked, he still didn't mention anything about coffins or graves, am I right?"

"We talked about them."

"Hold on there, Sheriff. Now, when you say *we* talked about them, don't you mean *you* asked him about them?"

"I did."

"He never brought up the matter of coffins or graves, did he?"

"No, he didn't."

"In fact, he denied ever seeing a coffin or grave, even in the dream he told you about, am I right?"

"That's right."

Tony, standing at the lectern, pointed toward the tools leaning against the prosecution's table. "Would any farmer here in Clermont County with a shovel and pick in his truck bed be a suspect for grave poaching?" Tony, smiling broadly, asked.

"Objection."

"Overruled."

"Of course not," I answered.

"You didn't take mud samples from these crime tools, as you call them, and the grave sites, did you?"

"No."

"You didn't, because mud is mud throughout Clermont County, isn't that so?"

"Objection."

"Sustained."

I noted smiles popping up around the courtroom. I didn't see anything funny about embarrassing an elected official in public.

"Well, doesn't mud on a shovel mean the shovel's been put to use?" Tony asked.

"That'd be the inference to draw," I answered.

Tony kept hopping all over from topic to topic. I kept to Bob's instructions to answer with as few words as possible. Those instructions might sound good to the attorney, but the witness on the stand can't take much comfort in them. Bob should have been objecting more to give me some breathing room from Tony's interrogation. I knew I could have done better without Bob's advice; but Bob was the prosecutor, and I was the sheriff. I wouldn't have taken orders from him during my investigation. I hadn't called him until after I had closed my case with the arrests of Lou and Duke for a reason.

For Tony's cross-examination on Lou's statement, Tony came at me from a different angle. "Didn't Lou tell you he was joking?"

"No, not exactly. He said he might say in court he was joking."

"He said he might testify that his statement to you was a joke?"

"I guess you can say that."

"Didn't he tell you he'd drop the biggest bomb ever dropped on Clermont County?"

"I think he did. Yes, he did. But he also said he did rob the graves."

"Was he joking when he told you that?"

I paused because I thought Tony might be baiting me with a trick question.

"Was he joking, in your opinion?" Tony asked again.

"No."

"Was he joking when he said he was joking, in your opinion?"

"Yes."

"So he told you he might say he robbed the graves, but he also told you he might say he was joking?"

"He did say both."

I couldn't say anything else.

After my testimony, Judge Flynn called out a recess. As I stood, I felt sweat coldly clinging my shirt to my back.

After the recess, Bob called Clara Jeffries and Todd Cobbler to the witness stand before resting the state's case in chief. Clara was glowing with self-importance. She added nothing to the case. She just confirmed my arrests of Lou and Duke and my seizure of the pocket watch. I think Bob called her just to add another body to the state's list of witnesses—justice by weight or volume.

Todd Cobbler called himself a dealer in antiques, old artifacts, and pre-owned jewelry. He was one of the oldest pawn brokers along the Ohio River, Illinois side. Despite his shoddy reputation, even he couldn't stretch the value of an old gold-plated pocket watch over one hundred and fifty dollars, the dividing line between misdemeanor and felony theft. Without seeing the other jewelry described in Lou and Duke's statements, he could offer only a nominal value.

After the state introduced its physical evidence—pocket watch, tools, belt, shoes, and photographs—and rested, Judge Flynn adjourned for the day. The crowd was waiting for Lou and Duke to testify. I hoped the jurors saw through the legal mazes laid down by the lawyers. The trial boiled down to me against Lou and Duke.

Chapter 13

THE next morning, the courtroom was buzzing. The reporters and public appeared more excited about Lou and Duke's testimony than they were about mine. After court was called to order, Judge Flynn called on the defense.

Tony stood. "Your Honor, I call Raymond 'Duke' Samms to the stand."

All eyes fell on Duke. At the same time, Duke's eyes fell upon his big hands knuckled up in a mound before him on the table.

"Duke," said Tony, as he tapped him on the shoulder and pointed to the witness stand.

He rose and walked slowly over to the stand. He eased his big frame down onto the witness stand. His body barely fit between the arms of the black walnut chair. On the stand, he sat stiffly in his blue denim jacket. He wouldn't even glance around the room. He stared straight ahead at Tony. The television artists began sketching him as soon as he sat down.

"What's your name?" began Tony.

"Raymond Samms."

"Do you go by another name?"

"Duke."

"Which name do you prefer?"

"Duke," he answered, with a sliver of a smile.

"Who gave you that name?"

"Lou."

"This Lou in court?" Tony asked, pointing at Lou.

"Uh-huh."

"Yes?"

"Yes."

131

"Are you and Lou friends?"

"Yep, we're partners."

Duke smiled. Lou's eyes wouldn't turn toward Duke. Duke was beginning to relax.

"Duke, tell the ladies and gentlemen of the jury where you're from."

"Jolly-et," he again pronounced it, "Illinois."

"Where's that from here?"

"North."

"Where north?"

He shrugged his big shoulders.

"You have to answer in words for the court reporter," Tony reminded him. "Where?" Tony continued.

Duke squinched up his forehead. "South of Chicago, by the jail," he answered.

"Do you have family there?"

"No."

"Where in Joliet did you live?"

"Objection," called out Bob.

"Counsel?" Judge Flynn asked Bob.

"May I have a sidebar?" Bob responded.

Judge Flynn marched off the bench to the side of the courtroom by me. The attorneys and court reporter followed.

"What does this testimony have to do with the crimes?" began Bob.

Judge Flynn looked at Tony.

"Judge, I'm going to show the jurors Duke's wayward childhood, which lacked any family structure or education, to give the jurors a view of his basic mentality, one totally dependent upon and susceptible to a dominant figure."

I didn't flinch and kept acting like I couldn't hear their conference.

"That'll take all day," said Bob.

"It might," said Tony.

"Is that your defense theory, Tony?" asked Judge Flynn.

"Yes, Judge, for Duke."

"You can proceed then, but you tie up this testimony with times, dates, places, and names for foundations."

"Thank you. I will."

The three returned to their places. The court reporter tagged along behind them.

"May I proceed, Your Honor?" asked Tony.

"You may, counsel."

"Duke, how old were you when you lived in Joliet?"

"When?"

Tony tried to set him back on track. "Let me put it to you this way, how long did you live in Joliet?"

Duke nodded. "Until I went to jail."

Bob grinned and looked at the jurors. A few jurors were smiling, but I couldn't tell what their smiles meant.

"How old were you then?"

"Eighteen."

"Who did you live with until then?"

"My mom."

"What was her name?"

"Joanne."

"Did she work when you were a little boy?"

"As long as I remember, she worked. She left me things to eat in the icebox."

"What kind of work did she do?"

"She told me sales. She left every night after supper. I always fell asleep before she came home."

Tony stepped back from the lectern. "Did your mom ever punish you?"

"Sure."

"What did she punish you for?"

"Messin' up the apartment."

"What would she do to you?"

"She slapped me in the face or locked me in my room."

"How long would she lock you in your room?"

"Sometimes, all night."

"Did you ever strike her back?"

"Hit Mom? No, never. I wouldn't hit Mom."

"Did you ever hate your mom when she punished you?"

"No, never. She was helpin' me. I'm slow at learnin' things. She helped me."

"She helped you by punishing you?"

"Yep, I didn't know better. I miss Mom." He started to dream.

"Duke, where is your mom today?" Tony asked softly.

"She's dead." He was staring into his hands and drifting off back in time.

"When did she die?"

"She died when I was in jail."

"How'd you find out?"

"I got a letter from a lawyer after she was buried. The lawyer wrote to tell me she was dead and no money was left after payin' the bills."

"Do you know how she died?" Tony almost whispered.

"Some kind of an accident."

"What about your dad?"

"I never seen him."

Tony paused. That courtroom was quiet. Bob wasn't grinning at the jurors anymore.

Before Duke's testimony, the jurors had been staring at big Duke peculiarly, like he was a captured beast. They had probably been expecting him to sound like some sort of demon. The more he talked, though, the more that expectation and perception slowly faded.

After several seconds passed, Tony asked him questions about his problems in school and with the law. He was first held back a few grades but then finally put in special classes for slow learners. In high school, he was placed in a trade program. He didn't finish the third year.

He didn't care for sports. A coach tried to interest him in football, but he didn't like hitting the other school kids on the field.

He worked a few jobs, packing and loading. His favorite job was cleaning up at a gas station. He liked to watch all the different cars pull in and out for gas. He never held any job long. He was never fired. The businesses closed, or he was let go for lack of work.

After he dropped out, he met Carlos. Carlos was always looking for something to do. He didn't especially like Carlos, but Carlos always looked him up when nobody else did.

Carlos played tricks on him. Most of the time, he wound up getting arrested—usually, for theft. Finally, Carlos picked him up late one night. Carlos wanted him to go for a ride in a car his friend let Carlos borrow. He suspected Carlos was playing another trick, but he believed he couldn't get in trouble for being a passenger.

The police arrested them for theft of an automobile and possession of a stolen automobile. He took the advice of an assistant public defender and pleaded guilty to possession for two years in the Illinois Department of Corrections.

In prison, he met Lou. He remembered the first time he met Lou. An inmate had slapped Duke in the face. He didn't know the reason. He didn't think he had done anything wrong. That's when he heard somebody shout at the inmate. The man was Lou. Lou was half their sizes, but Lou still shouted at the other inmate to find something better to do with his hands. The inmate turned on Lou, but Lou outboxed him with talk. The other inmate finally gave up on both of them and walked off.

They got to talking about things—charges, food, release dates, and plans. They started hanging together every day. He told Lou he had no plans, no place to go, and nobody to see. He remembered Lou's promise.

Duke looked up at the courtroom ceiling and captured a vision.

✳ ✳ ✳

"Now, listen here, Duke. This is the way it's going to be. I get out a week before you do. I got plans, plans big enough for two. I ain't in no rush, see? So here's what we'll do. You remember where that gas station is where you used to clean up? That's where I'll meet you the first Friday you get out, at six sharp. You got it?"

He smiled as he told their plan to the jurors. Now, he had a plan, a place to go, and somebody to see. He stumbled forward before the jury, as he described his vision.

That Friday, he stood on the corner in front of the gas station like he was told to do. A light rain fell. He got there a little after six. He checked the clock in the gas station, hoping he hadn't missed Lou. He waited and rechecked the clock. He waited some more and checked the clock again. Almost an hour later, a block down the street, he saw a man walking toward the gas station. The man was walking slowly but getting closer and closer. A half block away, he saw the man was Lou. He waved his big hand back and forth above his head. He kept waving until Lou walked across the street and up on the same corner he stood on.

"Sorry I'm late, partner," Lou said, "but I looked all over town and settled for these." Lou handed him a submarine sandwich and a can of pop. "I thought you'd be hungry, a big guy like yourself."

He thanked Lou for not forgetting him.

"Listen Duke, you got to learn something. I ain't got much, but I got my word. It ain't much, but it's mine and now yours. We're partners. What the hell would you do if I hadn't showed up anyhow?"

He had no answer. He hadn't thought about that because he didn't want and didn't have to.

"Well, you forget it, because I did show up. What's putting off my plans for a week?"

They walked over to a bus stop bench to eat their dinner.

✵ ✵ ✵

Duke's gaze dropped back down into the courtroom frozen in silence.

After Duke had told his vision, Tony took him through years of travel with Lou, running south to escape the winter and climbing back north in search of jobs. Although Lou kept putting off his plans—first a couple of days, then months, and finally, years—their partnership continued through four years of wandering.

Tony finally arrived at the point in time when they met me under Bender Creek Bridge. He skipped right over the crimes. I figured he was up to some legal maneuvers.

From the arrest, Tony took him to the statements. "You heard the sheriff tell the jurors in court about a conversation he had with you in his office, didn't you?"

"Yep."

"Do you remember that conversation?"

"Yep."

"During that conversation, you didn't tell him you robbed graves, did you?"

"Objection, leading," Bob called out.

"Sustained."

"Did the sheriff ask you if you robbed any graves?"

"Yep."

"What did you say?"

"I didn't see no graves."

"And you didn't tell him you stole the pocket watch out of a grave, did you?"

"Objection."

"Sustained."

"Did the sheriff ask you where you got the pocket watch?"

"Yep."

"You told him Lou found it, right?"

"Objection, Judge. I ask you to admonish counsel for repeatedly leading this witness."

Judge Flynn looked at Tony. "Mr. Pinelli, would you refrain from using leading questions in your direct examination?"

Tony nodded back. He'd gotten through to Duke. The jurors didn't seem to care what form of questions were asked. "Duke, what did you tell the sheriff about the watch?"

"I told him Lou said he found it and gave it to me."

"Let me show you some exhibits," Tony continued.

Tony stepped over to the prosecution's table, picked up the pocket watch, and then walked up to Duke. Tony held the watch out in front of Duke.

"I'm showing you People's Exhibit Number 1. Do you know what it is?"

Duke's eyes lit up. He reached for it, but Tony pulled it back.

"That's it."

"What's it?"

"The watch Lou gave me."

"What did you do with this broken pocket watch?"

"Sleep on it."

"You listened to it tick until you fell asleep?"

"Yep."

"Where did Lou get the watch?"

"He found it. He told me."

Tony switched watches behind his back. Duke's head tilted.

"I'm showing you Defense Exhibit Number 1. Do you know what it is?"

"The watch the sheriff gave me."

"When?"

"After he took my watch away." Duke tried to look around Tony to see the pocket watch Tony had clasped in the palm of his hand, behind his back.

"Did you use it to sleep too?"

"Yep. Lou says I wound it too hard. I busted it."

Tony walked back to the lectern after setting the watches back on the prosecution and defense tables. He was controlling Duke better than I expected. "Has Lou ever hurt you?"

"Nope, never."

"Has he hit you?"

"Nope."

"Has he ever yelled at you?"

"Yep, plenty of times."

Duke smiled and looked over at Lou. Lou looked away. Probably feeling he had done wrong, Duke wiped the smile from his face. "Lou helps me. He says he's got brains for both of us. I don't learn too good. He yells to help me. I know that. I got muscles for us both, though. Lou says so."

"Has he ever lied to you?"

"Nope, never since he met me at the gas station. His word is all he's got, all we got. What he says is so."

"Remember when you told us about meeting Lou in jail?"

"Yep."

"Does he always watch out for you?"

"Yep, always."

"Do you trust him?"

"I trust him."

"Do you do what he tells you to do?"

"Yep."

Tony again walked up to Duke after stepping next to the prosecution's table, but this time, he carried the tools. "I'm showing you People's Exhibits Numbers 2 and 3. Do you know what they are?"

"Yep, tools."

"Have you seen these tools before?"

"Yep."

"Where?"

"In our truck."

"Whose tools are they?"

"Me and Lou's."

"How do you know these are yours?"

"They look like 'em."

Tony walked back to the lectern after resting the tools against the prosecution's table. "Have you dug with the pick and shovel?"

"Yep."

"When was the last time you dug with them?"

"I don't remember."

"Well, didn't you talk to the sheriff about digging?"

"Yep, I did."

"What'd you tell the sheriff?"

"I was dreamin'."

"You told the sheriff you were dreaming about digging?"

Duke's head tilted. "Yep, I was dreamin' 'bout diggin'."

"What did the sheriff say?"

"He asked me to tell him about the diggin'."

"What did you do?"

"I told him."

"You told the sheriff you dug in your dream where Lou pointed, right?"

"Objection, Judge. He's leading again."

"Sustained."

"Where did you dig in your dream?"

"Where Lou pointed."

Bob just shook his head. Tony must have been doing really good.

"When you dug in your dream, was it night or day?"

"Night."

"Light or dark?"

"Dark."

"Real dark?"

"Objection."

"Sustained."

"Were there any lights where you dug?"

"Nope, none."

"How did you dig in the dark?"

"Mostly by feelin'."

"Could you see anything?"

"Nope."

"How long did you dig in your dream?"

"I don't know."

"When did you stop?"

"Lou told me to stop when I hit somethin' hard."

Tony paused a moment to act like he was collecting his thoughts. I think he knew exactly what he was doing and paused for effect, to catch the jurors' attention. "Did you climb out of the holes then?"

"Objection."

"Sustained."

"What did you do then?"

"I climbed out of the holes."

"Did Lou climb in the holes in your dream?"

Bob didn't bother to object.

"Yep."

"What did you do?"

"I took a rest and waited for him down by some crick or tree."

"Did you ever see what he did in the holes?"

"Nope."

"Did he ever tell you what he did in the holes?"

"Nope."

"How many times in your dream did you dig like that?"

Duke bobbed his head once, twice—

"Was it three?" Lou cut in.

"Yep."

"Three?"

"Three."

"Didn't Lou tell you in your dream that you were playing a trick like Halloween?"

"Objection, Judge, and another admonishment, please?"

"Sustained. Mr. Pinelli, I don't think leading is proper at this point in your direct examination."

Tony nodded. "Did Lou tell you anything in your dream?"

"Yep."

"What did he tell you?"

"We was playin' a trick like Halloween."

Tony must have said the word *dream* a dozen times. I'm pretty sure he was hoping to persuade the jurors' minds through repetition. Tony turned to a different subject. "Did Lou ever show you some jewelry?"

"Yep."

"When?"

"In the mornin'."

"Where?"

"In the truck in Paducah."

"Did he say how he got them?"

"Found 'em."

Tony wasn't flushing out too much detail with Duke. I don't know that he could. Probably more importantly, Tony didn't lose him any part of the way. Tony took him to Paducah where they found a pawn shop. Lou pawned the jewelry but gave the pocket watch to Duke. They bought some square meals and a bottle of whiskey for Lou.

"After Paducah, where were you and Lou going to go?"

"Home."

"Joliet?"

"Outside Joliet, so as I couldn't get us into trouble."

"Did you have plans?"

"Lou had plans big enough for both of us."

"Did he ever tell you those plans?"

"Yep."

"When?"

"'Round our fires at night."

"What were you two going to do?"

"Put down roots."

"What's that mean?"

"I don't know. He used to say it when he told me our plans at night. I liked to hear him tell me our plans. He'd look off into the night and smile."

Tony let Duke drift off. His dream was capturing everybody in the courtroom, jurors, reporters—even Bob.

"We was gonna have a home like everybody else, with beds and sheets and pillows and an icebox full of food we could open whenever we wanted. We was gonna go into business and open a corner tavern for anybody to come in and just talk if they wanted. Lou told me we'd call it Duke's." He smiled. "I like that, Duke's. Lou always done things for me. He never ate food without splitting it. If we had three apples, Lou gave me two. He said it was 'cause I was bigger. That's the way we done things. We're partners, Lou and me."

I glanced at Lou. His eyes were riveted on Duke.

Tony concluded, "Were you on your way to Joliet when you stopped at the general store in Greens Point?"

"Yep."

"That's when the sheriff here locked you up?"

"Yep."

Duke's dream broke off. He looked down into his hands on his lap.

"No further questions, Your Honor."

The courtroom fell silent. Some people looked at me. It was the darnedest thing. I had never felt that way before. I felt sorry for Duke and a bit guilty, though I knew full well I had done the right thing by locking him up.

After Tony sat down, I couldn't glean very much from his direct examination. The word *dream* was still echoing in my mind. Even if the jurors set aside Duke's dream, Duke had only testified to some digging for Lou and Lou pawning some jewelry he said he'd found. I figured Tony had done what he could with Duke's limitations. Tony's strategy would be tested by Bob's cross-examination.

Bob walked hesitantly up to the lectern. I suppose an attorney's script is a whole lot looser on cross-examination than direct examination. Poor Bob didn't have much of anything steady to grasp onto in front of that crowded courtroom, besides the lectern.

"Did you or did you not dig up three graves?"

I figured it was about time the attorneys got down to business.

"I dug up no graves."

Bob pulled back his thin hair. "Didn't you tell the sheriff, sitting across from you, that you dug up graves with Lou?"

"Nope. I never told nobody that."

"Did Lou tell you not to say you dug up any graves?"

"Nope. Lou never said nothin' 'bout graves."

Bob drew in a deep breath. He was throwing some hard punches, but they weren't landing too well. "Did you dig with these?" Bob approached Duke with the shovel and pick.

"Objection, Your Honor," called out Tony. "I'd like some foundation for Mr. Hunt's questions. I'd like Mr. Hunt to clarify his questions by directing Duke's attention to the digging in his dream or any digging he may have actually done."

"Judge," began Bob, "the state is not conceding to the dream defense. I don't have to concede to the defense to cross-examine."

"Mr. Pinelli," responded Judge Flynn, "Mr. Hunt will be allowed to cross-examine after laying a foundation for the conversation this witness had with Sheriff Carter."

Bob nodded.

"Thank you, Your Honor," Tony said.

"During your conversation with Sheriff Carter," continued Bob, "where did you say you dug?"

"In my dream."

"Where in your dream?"

"I couldn't see where. It was dark."

"Was Lou with you?"

"Lou and me."

Bob stopped for a moment. He must have felt he was getting on track and wanted to stay on track. "Did Lou tell you where to dig?"

"Yep."

"How many times?"

Duke's eyes looked up at the ceiling.

"Three, wasn't it?" Bob cut short.

"Yep."

"Three?"

"Three."

"What did you dig up?"

"I don't know."

"You don't recall?"

"I don't—know."

"Did you see anything in the grave?"

"Objection, Your Honor." Tony jumped up. "Duke testified he dreamed he dug but never dug any graves. There is no testimony tying Duke to the graves."

"Sustained."

That Tony was getting pretty picky. Despite a bumbling start, I thought Bob was finally starting to break through to Duke. "Did you see anything in the holes?"

"Nope."

"Did you feel anything?"

"Somethin' hard."

"What was it?"

"I don't know. I couldn't see it."

"How deep did you dig?"

"Deep."

"How big was this hard thing you hit?"

"I don't know. That's when I climbed out and Lou climbed in."

"Where did you go?"

"By a crick or tree to wait for him."

"Which creek?"

"Some crick."

"Did you see what he was doing?"

"Nope. I was by some crick."

"How long did you wait for him?"

"I don't remember."

"Can you say how long in minutes?"

"Objection, Your Honor. I don't know if anybody dreams in minutes."

"The witness may answer, if he can," Judge Flynn ruled.

"Let me rephrase the question," Bob offered. "Can you estimate how many minutes you waited for Lou while he was in the hole?"

"Nope."

Bob moved on. "What happened next?"

"Next?"

"Lou met you by the creek, right?"

"Yep."

"Did he show you anything?"

"Nope."

"Did he say anything?"

"Yep."

"What'd he say?"

"It's time to skedaddle."

Bob's cross followed them to Paducah through the pawn shop, meals, and Lou's bottle of whiskey. He got a description of the jewelry without the word *gold*. Tony objected to Bob's assumption of gold without introduction of the jewelry into evidence in court and Duke's inability to give an opinion that the jewelry was definitely gold. Nevertheless, Bob had two watches in court.

Bob approached Duke. "When did Lou give you this watch?"

Bob handed him the pocket watch. He stared at it in the palm of his hand.

"When did Lou give you this watch?" Bob repeated.

"Paducah."

"He gave it to you in Paducah?"

"Yep."

"Where'd the watch come from?"

"Lou says he found it."

Bob was on track with him but was going nowhere. He tried showing him physical evidence to shake something loose out of him. "Did you ever see Lou wearing these?" Bob held up the brown shoes and belt.

"Yep."

"Where?"

"Paducah."

"Where did these clothes come from?"

"Lou says he bought 'em."

"Did you see him buy them?"

"Nope."

"Then how do you know he bought them?"

"'Cause Lou said so."

"What if he said he found them?"

"He found 'em."

The longer cross-examination continued, the more tired Duke and Bob grew. Bob's cross drifted off into general inquiries. He accomplished nothing but boring the jurors and steaming Lou.

Perhaps in frustration, Bob took a gamble. He flashed a photograph of an open grave before Duke. Duke's face twisted, and his whole body shook. Lou almost sprang out of his chair.

Judge Flynn called out a recess. I glanced at my watch to see that the lunch hour had snuck up on us. I looked across the courtroom to see the jurors still staring at Duke. They appeared to be waiting for his recovery before leaving the courtroom for lunch.

Chapter 14

I HAD John watch Lou and Duke while I slipped over to Tucker's to try to get a table for a fast lunch. Even though I was Tucker's steadiest customer, I still couldn't get a table. The crowd from court flooded over to the bar and grill. I sat on a stool at the end of the bar.

After I ordered pulled pork, the reporter with the weasel face stepped next to me.

"Do you like Samuel or Sam, Sheriff Carter?" the reporter asked me.

"Sam's what my friends call me."

"Then Sam it'll be. You testified well the other day."

"Thanks," I replied but figured he was setting me up to pump me for more information.

"Tony Pinelli's as sharp as they are in Chicago," the reporter continued.

"Tony's all right. I couldn't say about Chicago lawyers."

"You didn't take mud samples?" the weasel asked, chuckling out loud.

"Of course not."

"He scored some points about the tools and statements."

"Lawyers are paid to score points, regardless of the truth."

"By the way, what did you order?"

"Pulled pork sandwich and chips."

"Hmmm."

The weasel tried again. "Duke is far from the graveyard monster we were all expecting."

"I'm sorry if you're disappointed. We have to take what we find down here. Monsters are hard to come by out here in the country."

"The jurors are warming up to him. They're starting to feel sorry for him."

"I'm not saying that, and your paper better not say I did."

"I still haven't decided if Duke is dumb or dumb like a fox. What do you think?"

"Dumb. Plain dumb."

"Fine, Sheriff. Do your duty. Here comes your sandwich."

The weasel walked back to his corner table where the other reporters were sitting. Jessie must have fit in well with that noisy lot. I finished my lunch and returned to court for Lou's testimony.

As the trial continued, the outcome seemed to shift more and more onto the shoulders of Lou. No witness had been seriously injured. Neither side had committed a major blunder. During Bob's cross-examination of Duke, I detected Lou growing visibly angry. Of course, I had training and experience in such observations in my line of duty. By the end of the cross, Lou turned red in the face, and two big veins on his neck and forehead were pumped out. He was a time bomb sitting in court, waiting to take the witness stand and explode.

There was expectation in the air. Before court was called back into session, the reporters acted livelier, walking, talking, and laughing. After the jurors were seated, they looked around the courtroom and chatted, as if they were loosening up before the start of a big heavyweight bout. The jurors now had the gumption to eyeball Lou and Duke more than they had before.

Lou sat in his chair in his plaid shirt buttoned to the top, with his back rigid. His eyes almost burned a hole in the witness stand. In contrast to Duke's blank stare, Lou looked intense, like he was chomping at the bit, mulling over the bullets he was planning to spit out.

When court was called to order, a hush fell over the courtroom. Tony called Lou to the stand. As with Duke, Tony began the examination with Lou's upbringing. Tony had to pry the words out of him. Lou didn't want any sympathy from the jurors. On that point, he was right. He wasn't about to get any.

Lou testified about his past bluntly and bitterly. By the time he explained his rough high school years in Harvey, his disdain for the established order was apparent: his fight with the dean of boys who expelled him, his bitterness toward the jocks and socialites, and his resentment of the other students excited over their extracurricular activities—the school paper, the student council, and the pep club. The jurors throughout this portion of the examination sat as still and cold as marble tombstones.

His experiences in jail kept the examination rolling steadily down-ward. He was a thief. He stole anything, anytime, and anywhere. Tony brought out Lou's "problems with the law" to soften the blow from Bob's expected impeachment of Lou's credibility with his convictions. He was a veteran of the Illinois Department of Corrections many times over by the time he met Duke.

"Sure, I hollered at the big ass for messing around with Duke. Duke's big, but he causes nobody no harm."

"Weren't you concerned for yourself?" asked Tony.

"No. Let me tell you a secret we little guys got over them big guys. We know they won't smack a little guy. That'd look bad for them. They want to look like a tough guy, not a bully. I could've yelled anything at that big ass, and he wouldn't have hauled off and hit me."

"What about Duke?"

"What about him? Would he have fought? Well, let me tell you this. I ain't never seen him hit anybody. He doesn't know what to do with them big hands of his. Lucky for that asshole. Duke could've twisted his head off like a cap off a beer bottle."

"Did you promise to meet Duke after his release?"

"I don't make promises. I told him I would, and I did. He didn't have nothing. I mean nothing. He had a ma who never wanted him around, and she upped and died while Duke was in the joint with me. He had no money, no plans, nothing."

"So you met him?"

"I met him at that gas station. I had to. I ain't no creep. He can't watch out for himself. He needs somebody, anybody. I might not be much, but I was somebody to him."

Tony was taking Lou slowly through the questions to establish Lou and Duke's relationship. He must have thought, if it couldn't help Lou, it might help Duke.

"Were you two partners?"

"Yeah, I used to tell him that. We looked out for each other, kept each other company."

Duke grinned ear to ear at Lou.

"Did you two have plans?"

"Yeah, I guess you could call them plans. I didn't think we'd ever be able to make them come true, but he liked to hear me talk about them."

"What were they?"

"Well, first, see, we had to get on our feet. When we got on our feet, we'd stop drifting. I told him we'd go into business."

"What kind?"

"I figured a corner tavern. Even I can run a tavern—pour the drink and ring it up. We wanted a neighborhood joint for the boys to come in, just to have a beer and talk."

"Did Duke drink alcohol?"

"Never. I wouldn't let him."

"Did you?"

"Now and then. A shot and a beer, maybe, when it was hot."

"How were you going to get money for a down payment?"

"Jobs. We were looking for odd jobs."

"Were you able to find any?"

"No, but we could have."

Tony was running a smooth direct examination, so smooth that the jurors and I almost forgot about him as we listened to Lou. "You met Sheriff Carter under the bridge, didn't you?"

"Yeah. It was raining cats and dogs."

"What did you and the sheriff say?"

"We just talked small talk."

"Who did all the talking?"

"The sheriff and me."

"How come?"

"I don't let Duke talk. He might talk himself into trouble. See, he'll say anything you want him to, not to lie but for attention. Like I said, we look out for each other."

Duke grinned ear to ear again.

"Did you see the sheriff a second time?"

"Yeah, at the general store."

"How long after the first time?"

"A couple weeks maybe. That's when he arrested us."

"Where were you heading?"

"I was taking Duke up north."

"What did the sheriff arrest you for?"

"Grave robbing. Can you believe it? I got no roots, but I ain't crazy either."

The jurors were studying Lou really hard now. Most were concentrating on Lou's face. A few glanced over at Duke. They couldn't have seen anything there, because I looked at that blank face of Duke's too. Nothing seemed to register with that man. He showed nothing. I started to believe that the man was so slow he couldn't know right from wrong. Lou led him around from town to town, watching out for him. Duke followed Lou, believed in Lou, and just about lived for Lou's attention. To Duke, maybe right was what Lou said was right, not what the law says. Lou had given Duke more than the law had.

"Let's stop here a moment, Lou," Tony said. "After your arrest, did you talk to the sheriff?"

"Sure did."

"What did you tell him?"

"It was more like what did he tell me."

"What do you mean?"

"He kept telling me about these graves and asking me if I dug them up. He told me about them over and over until I nearly committed them to memory."

"Then what happened?"

"Then I told him what he told me."

"Why?"

"I was sick and tired of these pea-brained lawmen. They're as stubborn and narrow sighted as a mule with them thick, black leather blinders on. They keep plodding on and on and on. They got to be doing for the sake of doing. They'd rather keep investigating wrong than cut off the whole investigation. Do you know what I mean?"

Well, I should say, I've taken insults but not a shot in public by nothing but a wayward thief. That Lou had the jurors and reporters glancing over at me, as if anything he was saying was near the truth. That weasel-faced reporter flashed another smile my way.

"What did you tell the sheriff?"

"I told him everything he told me. Of course, he didn't realize I was telling him everything he told me. No, he was too busy investigating."

"Did you tell him anything else?"

"I sure did. I told him that, if he was going to continue with this fool ishness, I was going to drop the biggest bomb that ever hit Greens Point."

"What did you mean by bomb?"

"Joke, man!" Lou shouted. His eyeballs popped out, and the veins in his neck and on his forehead bulged out. "Joke!"

Lou, glowering, stared at me. Then he continued raving at the jurors and spectators on the public benches.

"This is all a big joke, the crimes, the arrests, and this trial. You people out there got me and Duke locked up and tried for robbing gold from graves. You've got it all wrong. We ain't the gold diggers. You are.

"Me and Duke don't want nothing but to be left alone. But you people take a couple tramps like us and crucify us, show us off like circus freaks, sell us in your papers and stores, and then step on us for your careers.

"In fact, you're glad those graves were dug up. You don't give a damn about the graves. Those graves have only made you somebody important. You've got reporters down here asking you questions and artists drawing your pictures. You've got more money flowing into your town than you've had in years.

"You country folk ain't no different from city folk, no matter what you believe or lead people on to believe. You just talk slower and act smoother. You're all out to make a fast buck. You want to get something for nothing. You're all the same."

The court reporter's fingers stopped typing for a moment.

"Duke and me may be sitting in front of the judge, but you're the guilty ones. You're the ones robbing those graves for whatever you can get out of them."

The courtroom froze. Tony sat down shortly after Lou began raving. Judge Flynn called a recess.

I have to admit that Lou started me thinking there for a while. I then came to my senses. He was a raving fool. I arrested him for robbing gold from graves, and he turned around and accused everybody else of shameful thoughts and deeds. I hoped Bob would cut him up on cross-examination, but I didn't expect much.

After a half-hour recess, Bob rose to cross-examine Lou. At the outset, Bob returned to Lou's "problems with the law" and reiterated with more particularity Lou's theft and felony convictions. After the jury heard the chain of convictions, his goose was cooked. I couldn't see how any reasonable juror could believe one word from his mouth.

Cross-examination only gave Lou more time to attack. Bob was honest as the day is long and hard working, too, but he was slow on his feet and monotonous. Lou would hit Bob three times squarely on the nose before Bob could raise his arms in defense.

"Did you or did you not rob the graves?" Bob asked.

"I told you. You robbed the graves."

"Did you tell Sheriff Carter that you robbed the graves?"

"I told the sheriff that I was joking."

Bob scored no points on that exchange. "But the shovel had wet mud on it, correct?" Bob asked.

"I can't recall, really, if the mud was wet or dry, probably wet, if it was raining."

"Never mind the weather. You do admit that the shovel had mud on it?"

"It sure wasn't gold."

Bob would peck away for admissions, but the admissions didn't amount to much. He got lost in the procedure and forgot the end—a conviction. I swear every lawyer I ever met gets so lost in the going that they take three times the time and money to get where they're going.

"Didn't you tell the sheriff to be easy on Duke because he didn't know better?"

"I did."

"Then you're admitting you two did do wrong?"

"No. I was protecting Duke the way I always do. See, Duke doesn't do right or wrong. He says and does what I tell him. I say I was joking. Duke says he was dreaming. The sheriff says we were stealing. That's two against one. The state ain't got no case here."

There Lou went again, trying to make me, a lawman, look bad against a couple of tramps.

Bob tried flashing a photograph of an open grave in front of Lou. Lou stared into it and then straight back into Bob's eyes.

After Lou began to answer the questions before Bob completely stated them, Bob sat down. Luckily, Bob sat down before he began to answer Lou's questions.

Chapter 15

H OLLYWOOD producers, I suppose, make movies about sensational trials because closing arguments during trials excite the jury by evoking passion, sympathy, hatred, and any other emotion strong enough to sway the jury and the general public. I have never yet seen a successful movie or trial based upon unsupported and outright insult. From Lou's testimony to Tony's cross-examination, the entire defense seemed to me to be based upon personal insults aimed at the state's star witness—me. I bolstered myself up for closing arguments.

Before court was called to order, the crowd sitting on the benches and standing around the benches and down the center aisle resembled the crowd that assembles at our church's strawberry social each spring. The only exception was that the strawberry social was held outside.

Everybody who was anybody in Greens Point was present. They looked cleaned and pressed. The mayor was standing in the center of the aisle. His hand rested on a second-row bench right off the aisle. If Judge Flynn hadn't reserved the first row of benches for the reporters and artists, the mayor would have had his hand on row one, seat one. Nobody could miss spotting him. On top of his huge size, the mayor was wearing a white suit lit up by a bright lavender necktie. Across the aisle, I had managed to slip Betsy in row two on the aisle. Wally Davis was penned up way back, last row, last seat, in a rear corner—a cockeyed view of history in the making.

In criminal trials, the prosecution can argue twice in summation of the facts and in rebuttal to the defense argument, because the prosecution carries the burden of proof beyond a reasonable doubt. The defense is allowed one argument between summation and rebuttal.

Arguments were set for after lunch. During the morning, the attorneys and judge chose the exhibits to go to the jury, prepared the jury instructions, and agreed on the rules to govern closing arguments.

In summation, Bob merely rehashed the evidence. He recited my testimony of the discovery and investigation of the crimes and the arrests of Lou and Duke, followed by the recovery of the proceeds, the tools of the crime, and statements. He tried to break his monotonous delivery by holding up the exhibits before the jurors.

Tony and I, as I've said before, were never really friends, but we weren't enemies. He attacked my integrity throughout his argument.

Tony began with a bang. He walked up to the jurors and held out photographs of the open graves.

"Scare tactics," he hollered out. "The prosecution wants to scare you into convicting Lou and Duke. But these photographs are as thin as the state's case."

He ripped the photographs in half and tossed them on the floor.

In reflex, Bob reached for his photographs marked as exhibits before realizing the torn photographs were merely pretrial copies given to Tony and were not part of the court file.

"Nobody likes to be made the butt of a joke," Tony continued, "and just the same and even more so, nobody should be convicted of a crime, big or small, upon a joke. Nobody is saying Sheriff Carter didn't do a good job investigating."

It was too late for apologies.

"But," he continued, "in his desire to fulfill his duty to you, the citizens of Clermont County, he forgot that he, too, was an ordinary citizen like you and me with a sense of humor. He didn't believe a man with no hope, no future, and thus nothing to lose could still have a sense of humor. If Sheriff Carter has anything to feel guilty about, it would be from pressing too hard for you, and in so doing being unable to distinguish fact from joke."

Some defense. I was guilty for not having a sense of humor.

Tony then went through Bob's case, pointing out supposed deficiencies. Despite the proceeds and statements, he asked the jurors to ask the state where the written and signed statements of Lou and Duke were. He asked the jurors to ask the state, knowing full well I couldn't respond with the reason after the close of all the evidence. In his question, he was calling me a liar, as if I would lie to seek convictions of two drifters, to save face in the community and my political position.

After attacking what Bob failed to produce, he attacked what Bob did produce. From the opening statement forward, he attacked the prosecution around the shovel. "Blood on a shovel may mean wrongdoing outside of work, but mud on a shovel means digging, work. No matter what the prosecution says, a muddy shovel means work."

He also didn't forget those not present in court for the closing arguments. "I wonder if the insurance company has honored Holy Hill's claim yet and paid the money to Mr. Haney. Further, I wonder if he is going to keep all of the money or share it with his gravedigger, Norman."

Tony then offered his case: two drifters—a dreamer too dumb to know right from wrong following a joker too bitter to forgive society for locking him out. "Fortunately for you jurors, none of you has come from nowhere and has nowhere to go, besides a creek bed under an old bridge. Perhaps Lou's unfortunate past bent his sense of humor beyond our sense of decency. But a joke is a joke, no matter how much or little money the joker has. Knowing Lou's past and the incredible charges, I'm sure you could see Lou joking with Sheriff Carter and thinking he'd be let on his way shortly."

Tony moved off hardship and sympathy for Lou nearly as fast as he brought them up. Lou certainly didn't evoke sympathy from me.

Duke, however, was different. Tony started off really well for Duke. "I'm sure each one of you has glanced at Duke at some point during this trial, whether he was sitting on the witness stand or behind the defense table. You've heard his slow speech. You've seen his blank stare. He's a big simple man. He is not sly or cunning. He can't conceive any fancy defense. He can't lie."

Tony smiled and turned his head back toward Duke. After the pause, he resumed. "He says he dreamed he dug with Lou one night. He says he never even saw a grave in his dream. He has no knowledge of the grave robberies. He can't be found guilty of these crimes. Guilt requires wrongdoing first and foremost. After wrongdoing, guilt requires knowledge of wrongdoing. Nobody testified that he or she saw Duke commit any wrongful acts. Duke certainly didn't. Duke doesn't even know of any wrongful acts he supposedly committed. You have also seen the operation of his weak mind inside that powerful body. You have repeatedly heard throughout this trial the way he needs to be led by another dominant person. For four years, that person was Lou. He did or said what Lou wanted."

Tony stopped for a second to point his finger at the prosecution's table. "After Duke's arrest, for one hour, the state's star witness, Sheriff Carter, was that dominant person. Duke told the sheriff about one vague dream. Sheriff Carter filled in most of the details. Duke said what the sheriff wanted. The dream was Duke's. The statement is the sheriff's. You can't convict Duke for dreaming."

A compliment couldn't hide Tony's baseless attack on my integrity. He shoveled nothing but flimflam at the jurors, standing face-to-face before members of his very own community.

He then warned the jurors to judge Lou and Duke separately upon the evidence presented against and for each. He especially asked them not to find one guilty by association with the other.

Near the end of Tony's argument, he took a cheap shot. I thought it was cheap, because even I knew that the prosecution need prove only the elements of the crimes and not motive for the crimes.

"Purpose separates a dog from a man, a good man from a bad man, a prosecutor from an innocent man. Lou and Duke have no purpose for raiding Holy Hill. They were just passing through Greens Point.

"I submit to you, ladies and gentlemen of the jury, an old gold-plated watch cannot be the motive for robbing three graves. Lou could have stolen the watch and clothes across the river far more easily than camping out with Duke for two or three nights in a graveyard and robbing three graves.

"Sheriff Carter and Bob Hunt, though, as elected officials, have a purpose for convicting two drifters for grave robbing. Sam Carter was elected to preserve law and order throughout the county by enforcing the laws, and Bob Hunt was elected to prosecute. You hold them to their burden of proof and have them explain to you the reason two drifters would dig up three graves in Southern Illinois."

Tony held his best argument for last. He dropped a bomb. "Ladies and gentlemen of the jury, you have heard a lot about statements and tools of the crime. I would like to close by calling your attention to the proceeds, not the gold-plated pocket watch with some engraved letters but the belt and shoes."

Tony stepped over, picked them off of Bob's table, and returned in front of the jury, holding the clothes out for the jurors to see. "Please take a look, a really good look, at these clothes. A one-hundred-year-old belt and shoes don't look like the belt and shoes you lost and found a year later at the back of your closet."

He paused and turned to the left and right for the jurors to view the clothes closer. "Leather is made from animal skin. Fabrics like wool or cotton are natural fibers. They can't last a century buried underground in a wooden coffin. The corpses were petrified. Their suits were decomposed. So what are we to conclude?" He waited a moment. "The conclusion: this belt and these shoes are from a store in Paducah—or—somebody's garbage along the way."

Tony dropped his arms. He paused again and then looked from left to right at the jurors. "Men in the 1800s wore suspenders, didn't they?"

He turned from the jurors and walked to set the clothes back down on Bob's table.

Bob started off in a deep hole. Although I've never sat as a juror, jurors look like they take their jobs seriously, being sworn and all. They aren't likely to forget or ignore important points raised in arguments, especially the big stuff. He made a huge mistake not touching Tony's strongest argument.

Bob's rebuttal was too rational. Just like in cross-examination, he pointed out inconsistencies that didn't amount to a hill of beans. He pulled out stock arguments. He tried coincidence. He raised his voice for planned effect and eased off after completion, but he moved forward with nothing.

"Do you honestly think Lou and Duke's possession of Jerome Taylor's pocket watch was a coincidence?" he asked the jurors. He was asking the jurors more questions than he was answering questions for them. "How about Lou's wearing a brown belt and shoes and the corpse of Henry Albrecht missing a brown belt and shoes?"

I'm not a lawyer, but even I know questions don't remove doubt. Answers do.

He stuck his neck out too far. I'm not saying he shouldn't have tried to explain motive, if he could have effectively. But I think he was able to swim only halfway across the river. The current then took him downstream and, in doing so, sent me down the river.

"The state doesn't have to prove motive. The judge will so instruct you. The state need only prove the elements of the crime beyond a reasonable doubt. Motive isn't an element."

The state should never apologize.

"But I'll tell you the reason Lou and Duke robbed those graves. You heard about their backgrounds and, mind you, I didn't say upbringings, because they didn't have any. Nobody ever taught them morals, religion, or right from wrong. They don't know right from wrong and just plain don't care about doing right."

He started off good, but he just dropped the topic and didn't bring it across to the jurors.

Bob dismissed Duke's dream defense as a lie. He likened Duke to a child quick to forget or say he forgot doing wrong. According to Bob, the similarities between the graves uncovered in my investigation and Duke's dream proved Duke had dug up the graves. Bob argued Duke could call his acts anything during the trial but knew at the time he was digging. Further, Duke could not escape guilt by limiting his involvement to digging. Lou and Duke were partners. Although Lou did the planning and Duke did the digging, both were equally guilty of grave robbing.

Regarding credibility, Bob hammered away at their convictions. He turned the tables on Tony by arguing that surely "those convicts" had a greater motive to lie and concoct defenses to escape convictions than I had to fabricate evidence. I wish Bob had pounded away a little harder on that point.

Bob then addressed the guts of Lou's defense at the end of his rebuttal. He did fine by me. "The defense concocted a joke defense. The joke defense was concocted because there was nothing left for Lou to say. The state has presented statements, proceeds, and tools for the crimes. He has no defense, so he concocts this bold face lie in the disguise of a joke. You heard Sheriff Carter describe the dug-up graves with the coffin lids broken open and the bodies decayed, eternal sleep attacked. Nobody in Greens Point will or can laugh at those cold facts of these terrible crimes."

Bob planned a pause before his big ending. Unfortunately, everybody in the courtroom, including the jurors, could feel his short and stiff stop and start and see his index finger tapping out one one thousand, two one thousand, three one thousand.

After three silent beats, he concluded: "Ladies and gentlemen of the jury, please remember one final point. If you fall for Lou's joke, Lou will be laughing at you all the way out of this courtroom."

Bob pointed his finger at Lou, dropped his arm, and walked to his seat. The reporters raced out of the courtroom into the hallway to make their telephone calls. Judge Flynn began reading the jury instructions shortly before dinnertime.

The wait began.

✳ ✳ ✳

I walked over to Tucker's and sat at the bar. I couldn't eat. I ordered a beer and nibbled on peanuts.

Over a big joke, I felt I was being sent down the river. If the jury returned a verdict of not guilty, the papers around the country would publicize the bomb dropped on Greens Point and destroy my reputation as a lawman. I had carried the town on my back from the investigation to the arrests. A lawyer got a hold of my work and turned it into a joke. He was getting paid for cracking a joke at my expense.

When I entered Tucker's, I saw Jessie Daniels laughing in the corner with that weasel-faced reporter and Matt Best out of Springfield. She was probably busy cementing her contacts with those big-shot reporters. I tried to avoid them, obviously, but they were reporters, without manners, and approached me anyhow.

"Are you a betting man?" asked weasel-face.

"No."

"I am. I'll bet you a beer the jurors vote guilty."

I turned to look at their faces.

"The jury's got nothing to lose by returning a guilty verdict and everything to lose by returning an acquittal," he continued. "This town doesn't have much, but it's got its pride and reputation. Whether those men committed the crimes or not, they're going down."

That's when I first thought I might have that reporter pegged wrong.

"Do you give interviews?" he asked me.

"Not to reporters," Jessie said.

"That depends on who's the reporter," I said.

"After the verdict, I'll come look you up. I might make it worth your while."

"You know where to find me."

"The sheriff's office or town hall?" Matt tossed in with a smile full of teeth.

"Not me, not now."

"I'll be expecting one of you to run for a seat in the legislature. How about Bob or Tony?"

"Ask them."

"You know I will."

They left me.

I made my way through the small bowl of peanuts and ordered another beer.

A couple hours later, John Day hobbled over to my stool. All eyes watched him. "Jury's got a verdict," he whispered in my ear.

When I stood, all the chairs in the place screeched back on the wooden floor.

"Verdict?" called out several voices.

I marched out the door, followed by John nodding his head.

The courtroom was dimly lit by sconces with open metal pans bent upward along the two long side walls. Vintage lights sealed in milk glass lit the ornate ceiling. After the crowd settled and the stage set for Judge Flynn, John called the court in session. Judge Flynn walked up to the bench to take his seat. A reading light on the bench lit up his face and surrounded the bench with shadows on the walls.

"Bring in the defendants," the judge said.

I nodded and brought in Lou and Duke, who took their seats before me. The courtroom held a dim glow with dark shadows caught in the upper and lower corners of the room. Duke still wore that blank stare. I wondered if he really understood his situation. In contrast, Lou looked bitter and foul. I knew he knew too well his situation.

A shudder ran down my spine. For lack of a better word, I felt an eerie sensation throughout the courtroom. Perhaps the sensation arose from the nature of the crimes. Perhaps the sensation arose from the basic act of judgment upon man. Regardless of the source, I shook off the cold sensation.

"Bring in the jury," the judge said.

John led the jurors in line into the courtroom to their seats. Most wouldn't look at Lou and Duke. After the jurors sat, Judge Flynn called to the foreman.

"Mr. Foreman, has the jury reached a verdict?" asked the judge.

"We have, Your Honor."

"Hand the verdict forms to the deputy sheriff."

Fred Tate, a grain elevator operator and a good sign for the prosecution, handed the verdict forms to John. John hobbled over to the bench and handed the verdict forms up to the judge. Judge Flynn read each verdict slowly to himself, put them in order, and then read them aloud.

"We, the jury, find the defendant, Lou Vitale, guilty of possession of stolen property."

The crowd was smiling and nodding. Old weasel-face was nodding at some of the other reporters, probably collecting his debts. That verdict, however, was a sure bet.

"We, the jury, find the defendant, Lou Vitale, guilty of theft."

That verdict should have been the clincher.

"We, the jury, find the defendant, Lou Vitale, guilty of destruction of a tomb."

Lou didn't flinch during the reading of his verdicts. He stared into his folded hands during the reading of Duke's. Everybody in the crowd sitting on the rows of benches looked at Duke. Only a few jurors did. Duke was definitely guilty of being stupid, but he didn't seem to have a mean bone in his body. His stupidity could have been his strongest defense.

Judge Flynn set down Lou's set of verdict forms and picked up Duke's.

"We, the jury, find the defendant, Raymond 'Duke' Samms, guilty of possession of stolen property."

Duke, too, was found guilty of all counts. I figured guilt by association but guilt nonetheless. After Judge Flynn read the verdicts, a few jurors peeked at Duke on their way out of the courtroom. He just sat there and stared at the judge. Judge Flynn became uneasy, looked away, and asked me to remove the defendants from the courtroom. I'm sure Duke didn't realize yet what the impact of the verdicts would be to his life or friendship with Lou.

As I tapped Lou and Duke on their shoulders to stand, Duke stood and looked at Lou. Lou looked straight away from Duke and led the three of us out of the courtroom to the holding cell.

I returned to the courtroom and congratulated Bob before he went into the jury room to thank the jurors. He was now loose and all smiles. I planned to walk outside to mill around with the crowd. I didn't get a chance because the reporters stopped me as soon as I stepped through the gates of the inner well of the courtroom into the center aisle between the public benches. I wish I hadn't sent Betsy home after the closing arguments, so she could have seen me surrounded by the reporters.

To reporters, I could only agree with the verdicts upon the evidence presented throughout the trial and the information learned through my investigation. I managed to state the effectiveness and value of the judicial system and law enforcement as demonstrated by Judge Flynn, Bob Hunt, and myself.

On the way outside, weasel-face whispered to me, "I might have said the town had pride and reputation, but I never said a word about a sense of humor."

Upon seeing Mayor Stubbs moving toward me through the crowd and probably wanting to have joint photographs with me taken for the *Bugler*, I slipped away from the courthouse. After I left the courthouse, I decided it was too late to stop off at Tucker's. The beers and the excitement from the verdicts were beginning to tire me. I expected Tucker's to be crowded and loud too. Instead, I stopped off at the office to check on Lou and Duke before I drove home.

By the time I was through with the reporters and arrived at the office, John had already locked Lou and Duke up, shut off the lights, and left. I flipped on the lights and walked in the back room to the cells.

Only light from the street lights fell through the cell windows. Lou was lying flat on his back. Duke was sitting up in the middle of his cot with his feet on the floor and his elbows on his knees.

"What are you doing up, Duke?" I asked him.

"Thinkin'."

"About what?"

"What's gonna happen to Lou and me."

"That's up to the judge. He can choose all kinds of sentences."

"Yeah, Duke," Lou broke in, "the worst he can do to us is toss us back in the joint."

"Is that so, Sheriff?" Duke asked.

"It's possible," I answered.

"I'd like that sentence," Duke said aloud to himself.

"You'll find out in a couple of weeks, so just go to sleep," I told him.

Duke didn't budge. "Sheriff?" Duke said.

"Yes."

"Can Lou and me have the same sentence?"

I knew what was beginning to bother him, but I didn't want to upset him. "It's like I already told you. You may, but you may not. It's up to the judge."

"I want the same sentence. We got us plans, Lou and me do. We're partners."

"Come on, Duke," hollered Lou. "Lights out. You heard the sheriff. We got to wait for the judge. It's all up to the judge."

Duke lay back on his cot.

"Good night, fellows."

"Good night, Sheriff," Duke said.

CHAPTER 15

After the trial, everything should have been fine. But it wasn't. I felt an uneasiness, a gnawing inside of me. Duke was starting to throw me and the system out of whack.

I drove home and talked to Betsy. I told her about Duke's desire to receive the same sentence as Lou. According to the law, Duke was convicted of crimes and should be punished regardless of his stupidity. But, according to Betsy, he was mostly guilty of needing somebody.

"Don't start judging anybody," she told me. "There's only one judge, and you know who I'm talking about." She kept up her defense of the downtrodden.

I didn't respond. How could I? She was the moral compass of our family and home, pointing our direction like a gravitating needle.

"Jesus raised Lazarus from the tomb," she continued. "I know you know the book of John. Do you know what Lazarus said?" She flashed those mysterious hazel eyes at me.

"Not right now, I don't. I recall Mary was there—and Martha—Jesus wept."

"Jesus wept?" She repeated, staring at me and waiting for me to look into her eyes.

"Yes, I'm pretty sure about that one."

After our eye contact hit, she looked away.

Betsy left it at that—questions. She wasn't even aware that she spoke in parables. Over our thirty years of marriage, Betsy always said life's lessons are better learned if you can find the answers yourself.

Chapter 16

THE next afternoon, Reverend Betts came to visit Lou and Duke. I suppose men of the cloth have duties somewhat like lawmen. Each has to do certain acts he'd rather not but must. I figured he had come over to determine if there was any hope for Lou and Duke. I figured time had run out for both.

The reverend went into the back room alone, so I don't know what was said. But I did talk to him on his way out.

"How are they doing, Reverend?"

"They act like they've adjusted to their present situation. I suppose they've grown used to jails."

"I suppose so."

"It's a pity what becomes of a lonely man, Sam. Loneliness changes each one differently. Some turn toward bitterness, some toward crime. If only we could reach them."

"What do you think of Duke?"

"He's luckier. His need is the stronger of the two."

The clergy seem to view the whole world differently.

"May I visit again?"

"You can stop in whenever you want."

I stopped him at the door. "How's the Horner estate?"

"Mr. Cain is completing the legal details for the transfer."

"Do you mind if I ask you what you'll be doing with the farm?"

"I'm still working out the details."

"Is Norman still out there alone?" I slipped in.

"He is."

"What do you think of him?"

"Ah, Norman," the reverend smiled. "At least, one lonely man has found the power of Scripture."

"I know he reads the Bible. He told me he finds answers to his problems in that old worn Bible of his."

"I suppose that's one way of saying it."

☆☆☆

Over the next few days, Reverend Betts visited with Lou and Duke. Not that I eavesdropped on their conversations, but once I overheard the reverend speaking with them. The door separating the hall of cells from the front office was open. I happened to be nearby. I heard but a slice of the three of them.

"Only God knows our destiny," said the reverend.

"Future, you mean future, don't you, Reverend?" snapped back Lou. "He means future, Duke."

"Future," repeated Duke.

"Christianity is the only faith that offers grace. You do not earn grace. Rules and practices are not steps that lead to grace. Grace is not measured by your past."

"Our pasts ain't too good, there, Reverend," cut in Lou.

"The history of the human race shows that we, too, have all failed again and again to listen to the word of God."

"History is when God speaks to us," mumbled Duke.

"Pardon?" the reverend said.

I'm glad the reverend broke in, because I hadn't heard what Duke had said.

"Don't mind him," Lou answered, "Duke talks to himself sometimes. It ain't nothin', never amounts to much."

"No. No. I'd like to hear what he said," replied the reverend. "Duke, what did you say to us?"

"History is when God speaks to us," repeated Duke. "My mom used to tell me that."

"That's deep, Duke. Let me think about that one. The Bible is a record of God's breakthroughs with humanity," the reverend acknowledged.

"Deep? I'll tell you what's deep," Lou broke in. "Sometimes, I wonder if the whole fuckin' world is crazy, or it's just me."

When I twitched from the f-word, my shoulder hit the door and the hinge creaked. Briskly, I took a step away and returned to my tasks.

✳ ✳ ✳

The day before sentencing, the reverend paid them a visit. He walked out of the hall of cells and sat down before my desk.

"Sam, what sentences do you think Judge Flynn will impose on them?"

"I can't say for sure, but I'd bet jail time for both. You see, Reverend, both are already convicted thieves: generally, the more convictions, the greater the sentence. All the crimes charged, however, were misdemeanors, which means a jail sentence must be less than a year with credit for time served before the sentencing hearing."

I could see in the reverend's face that he was thinking. I think he was trying to formulate his thoughts into words.

"What are Duke's chances at probation?"

"They're there. I can't say they're strong."

"What if he has a sponsor?"

Now, I could see the reverend's line. "The law's changed a bit. Nowadays, judges usually don't release defendants to a sponsor's custody. I'm not saying they won't. Why? Do you want him?"

"I could place him on the farm and, depending on how he does, keep him there or direct him to a social service through the church."

I wasn't used to dealing with a reverend. I didn't care for the bargaining angle. Like I said, the clergy seem to view the world differently. They appear not to listen too well either, I might add. Betsy had me pushing for Norman on the farm, and the reverend asked about Duke.

I was still having that uneasy feeling about Duke. I knew tossing him back into the system wouldn't do him or anybody else any good. He'd only fall to greater abuse. But probation for a defendant already convicted of theft didn't sit too well with me. "I'm not sure. Let me run that by Duke and the judge. I'll have to get back to you on that."

Later that day, I called Judge Flynn.

"Well, that's a surprise to hear coming from a lawman," answered the judge.

"I'm not recommending probation, Judge. I'm calling you because I told Reverend Betts I would."

"I know. I know. What do you think?"

"You're the judge. I'm not so sure considering his record, the nature of the crimes, and the town's reaction. I'd consider it, though."

"All right, fine. I'll think it over. You can tell Reverend Betts you told me. Do me a favor, Sam. Ask him to be in court for sentencing."

"I'll do that."

Judge Flynn belonged to our congregation. I guess it would have made no sense setting off our reverend. I knew, too, Judge Flynn was considering retirement after his term expired. To him, the community's reaction might not have been so important as the reverend's.

Throughout the week, I hadn't talked with either Lou or Duke much, except for an occasional hello. I did hear them talking back there in the lockup now and then. Of course, I didn't hear what they might have said during the night.

At the end of the day before sentencing, I walked back to their cells to have a talk with them. "How are you fellows feeling today?"

"Same as yesterday," snapped Lou.

"Tomorrow, you'll be sentenced."

They both remained silent.

"I don't know for sure, but I heard some talk that the judge may go easy on Duke."

Duke looked at Lou. He wanted Lou to say something. Lou didn't.

"I heard the judge may give Duke probation."

"Will the judge give Lou probation?" Duke asked quickly. He couldn't stay quiet any longer.

Lou laughed. "I stopped getting paper years ago," Lou said.

"Then I don't want paper either," Duke said.

Lou just smiled and shook his head.

Nobody said anything for a few moments. Finally, Lou looked up at me. "What kind of probation are they talking about for Duke?" Lou asked.

"The judge might place him outside of town on a farm owned by Reverend Betts."

"Good Samaritan Sheriff Sam," Lou began. "You all feel there's hope for Duke and none for me." Lou paused. "Well," Lou continued, "you may very well be right."

"Is Lou goin' to the farm too?" Duke asked.

"I'm going back to the joint, Duke."

The conversation began to move too fast for Duke. He just sat there and looked blank.

"You two can always write," I said.

Then I remembered Duke's limitation. But it didn't matter. There was no more getting through to Duke. Lou didn't want to hear anymore.

As I stepped out of the back room, I glanced at Duke's blank stare. Sometimes, I just don't understand myself. I felt the sharpest pain looking at him. As Betsy said after seeing him in court, he seemed so lost in the world. There two men sat in a lockup in Greens Point. Nobody outside of Clermont County ever heard of the place, until Lou and Duke put us on the map by robbing three graves. When I looked at Duke's blank stare, I felt just how big this darn old world is and how lost a man can be. The sensation was a bit frightening. It came and went with a flash. I felt as if he was sitting in the center of the world, alone, with a gripping need for somebody. He felt only a basic need. He wanted nothing more. His mind didn't operate in terms of money, power, or fame.

For the rest of the evening and long into the night, I felt confused. Betsy let me be. I still couldn't recall what Lazarus said. She knew I would have to work out this problem within myself. She and I always looked at problems from opposite sides. Our marriage, though, has been long and happy. Opposites do attract.

Near midnight, I fell back on reason to steer me through the mess my feelings had mustered up on me. I placed myself back into my role as the county sheriff sworn to uphold the laws of Illinois. At that point, I tried to piece together a solution for Duke and myself. As I neared the point, I fell asleep.

* * *

I awoke the next morning at ease. I realized the judge would probably side with Reverend Betts, and so should I. I couldn't gain anything by opposing a judge and preacher. I had more or less slept on the problem and let the problem work itself out. As I often have said, in time, problems solve themselves. Reverend Betts's suggestion was working itself into a solution.

At the sentencing hearing in the morning, the crowd had tapered off. The newspaper reporters had returned to their big cities. Sentences for misdemeanors aren't too severe. Only Jessie was present. I'm sure she had made deals with the reporters to relay the sentences to them.

Sentencing passed softly, after the climax of the jury verdicts. Reverend Betts was present to answer Judge Flynn's questions. Lou and Duke sat motionlessly throughout the hearing. Neither appeared to be listening. Duke didn't want to hear, and Lou didn't care.

They were called to stand before the bench for the judge to pass sentence. The judge asked each if either cared to make a statement.

Lou began. "Judge, the jurors had no sense of humor. With you coming from the same town, I figure you ain't got a sense of humor neither. I also figure I'll need one where you'll be sending me. I can't take anything else with me there. Do what you want with me. I been there before." Lou then reached over and placed his hand up on Duke's shoulder.

Duke smiled and looked down at Lou.

"But give the big guy a break. He's never had one in his whole life. Me, I couldn't afford to give him one. I looked after him the best way I could, despite what you all think. But you, Judge, you can afford to give him a break." Lou squeezed Duke's shoulder and smiled up at him.

Duke was smiling back at Lou until the judge asked Duke for his statement. Duke then turned and looked straight into Judge Flynn's eyes. "I want to go back to jail with Lou. Where he goes, I go. It's always been that way, and it'll always be that way. We're partners, Lou and me, ain't we, Lou?"

Duke looked at Lou, but Lou couldn't look back at Duke. Lou nodded his head slowly but kept his stare straight ahead into the wooden bench. Duke looked back at Judge Flynn.

Judge Flynn announced the sentences. He gave Lou three hundred and sixty-four days in jail, less time already served in custody. He gave Duke probation for one year under Reverend Betts's sponsorship with the time he had already served considered served as part of the sentence.

"Deputy," concluded Judge Flynn, "take the defendants away."

Lou walked off with John Day, but Duke stood staring at the judge.

"I don't want no probation," said Duke. "I want to go with Lou."

"I have passed sentence. Sheriff, take the defendant away."

I pulled on Duke's arm, and he followed. He was looking around the courtroom for Lou, who had walked back to the holding cell. "Sheriff, I don't want no probation."

"Let's go, Duke. The judge and reverend know what's best."

"What about Lou?"

"He'll come meet you again when he gets out just like before."

"We're partners."

"It's not even a year, Duke."

Back in the holding cell, Duke stood, staring at Lou through the cell bars. Lou, at first, wouldn't look at Duke. Finally, Lou walked over to Duke, reached through the bars, and grabbed his arms. "Listen, Duke. We're partners, ain't we?"

Duke nodded back.

"I take care of you, don't I?"

He nodded again.

"You'll listen to me then, won't you?"

He nodded.

"I'm telling you now to go with the sheriff. He's okay. He won't short-change you. Maybe I done you wrong. But I always did what I could for you. I could never give you a break. I never had one to give. I asked the judge to give you a break, and he did. I want you to get a break like everybody else gets at least one sometime." Lou wasn't getting through to Duke. Lou pushed harder. "And no matter what happens, we're still partners. We'll always be partners, me and you."

The last line got through to him. "We're partners, ain't we, Lou? And we'll always be partners no matter what."

"No matter what." Lou nodded and smiled.

"Let's go, Duke," I said, as I pulled on his arm to begin leaving.

Duke stopped. "Lou?" He asked.

Lou looked up.

"You're gonna meet me when you get out, just like last time, ain't you, Lou?"

"Don't I always take care of you? I always do the best I can for you, don't I?"

"Yep, you sure do."

"There. Now you go along with the sheriff. I'll wait here for my ride."

Duke smiled.

I pulled Duke away. Lou looked away from us. Duke drifted off from all that happened so quickly.

I had arranged for the reverend to promptly meet us at the office to take Duke away. Mostly, I couldn't bear the silence around the big fellow. I was afraid he'd realize what was happening to him.

✲ ✲ ✲

Autumn rolled around slowly and politely, as usual in Greens Point. The yellows, oranges, reds, and purples burst out and up before their fall. Of all the trees, the magnolia belongs to the South. The large waxed leaves fall from the cold, gray boughs to coat the ground like a wet, brown rug. As events tumble and years pass to decades, the magnolia, Cairo, and Little Egypt endure. Greens Point lived, died, and arose.

Life is bigger than the earth. There are so many different ways to look at life that nobody can see it all. One view from Greens Point can encompass life as big or bigger than a hundred views from Paducah or a thousand from Chicago.

Thirty-three murders by John Gacy are tucked away in newspaper articles. Lawyers, professors, and students will study the court opinions. I never read any of the articles, and I don't plan to read one opinion. I have no need to read them. I'm still trying to learn the lesson two drifters brought into town.

Within a couple years from the trial, a lot of changes happened around town. To start on a sad note, old Jeb got knotted up with rheumatism and died of pneumonia the winter following the trial. I'll miss Jeb's shuffling around the office. I doubt if Hank will miss him. Hank beat out Rusty for my old office of sheriff of Clermont County.

Voters elected Bob to become a judge and Tony to become a state representative. As the saying goes, "Strike while the iron is hot."

Judge Flynn and I announced our retirements. Professionally speaking, nothing bigger could culminate our careers. Although now the former law enforcement officer of the county, I still felt compelled to truthfully set the record straight. I sensed a duty to publish my manuscript to defend the good folks of Greens Point from any slanted attack any outsider may have attempted to put in writing. True history is based upon facts.

Jessie Daniels finally moved on, or up as she preferred to call it, to Chicago, to join the weasel at the *Sun Times*. She was a funny woman. I could never understand what drove her. Her last words to me didn't help much either: "If you don't like things, change them. If you can't change them, move on." I never claimed she was a hypocrite. That's, in fact, what she did. To me, that type of sediment is too unsettling. I suppose we just didn't see anything the same way, two different honest opinions. We were opposites. That was all. Her departure was the best for both of us.

The trial turned the tragedy from the graves into a blessing for the town. Not only did the publicity add fuel to a few careers, but it generated money for the local businesses. The notoriety from the crimes and trial helped Greens Point become a stopover for one of the renovated steamboat lines hauling sightseers and vacationers up and down the Ohio River.

Tucker's gained a seasonal influx of new customers. Tucker even changed his menu a bit to cater to them. After a few inquiries from tourists, Clara started setting out old pieces of furniture for sale by the bags of seed and fertilizer in front of the general store. She was doing pretty good selling those antiques, as she began calling them, especially to the big-city customers. Even Tommy started a side business from the gas station, driving tourists from the pier up to town and back in a van he refurbished. Should business continue to grow and Greens Point were to land a sleepover, some of the townsfolk started talking about converting their homes into bed-and-breakfast inns. Now, that's Southern hospitality. The bustling about town rekindled tales from the golden days. After over a century, the jewel along the Ohio was beginning to sparkle once more.

Even though I, above all, deserved a share of any benefit from the crisis, I decided to retire at the end of my term and write this account of the grave robberies. All the publicity hadn't turned my head. I kept my chronicle close to my eyes and ears to reflect an accurate record of the events that could have toppled Greens Point. If anybody could put order into history, that would be me. After all, the residents of Little Egypt deserve to stand out in their little slice of history.

"I give up," I told Betsy one evening. "I don't remember. After Jesus raised Lazarus from the tomb, what did Lazarus say?"

The ceiling light shined down on her sitting at the dining room table with her Sunday sheet music spread out. Sometimes green, sometimes light-brown, on this very rare occasion gold, she raised her hazel eyes up from the stanzas and notes, fixed her eyes on me, and smiled.

"Nothing. Absolutely, nothing."

There she went again—stirring the pot but not calling me home for dinner. I just shook my head. I'd have to sleep on that one. I hoped time would tell me the answer.

The only people who I can think of who didn't get anything from the trial would be Duke and Norman, except they were more or less outside of town. The publicity from the trial hadn't even scratched their lives. Gently as I can say it, their lack of intellect barred them from the benefits that the rest of Greens Point was enjoying.

CHAPTER 16

I stopped in at the Horner estate to visit Duke and Norman. The church had those two big oxen under the yoke, tilling up the fields once again. Instead of decent wages, the reverend was probably giving them room and board, spending money, and Bible instructions. They appeared to be getting along. Both were too simple to be able to quarrel. The reverend moved them both inside the house. Norman's shed was turned back into the henhouse.

Lou returned to jail. The self-proclaimed joker of the biggest whopper wound up the fool. He had tried to turn the town into the butt end of a joke during the trial. In my opinion, though, the trial put the town one up on little Lou. The brains of that partnership wound up behind bars, with the muscle getting a break on probation. I never thought he was too smart. He was one of the bitterest little men I ever ran across. His slander of the citizens of Greens Point from the stand was pure nonsense. Our citizens are simple, hardworking people. The proof is in the pudding. Our town is moving back to its golden days, and Lou is off somewhere else finding shelter under a bridge.

At times, during the trial and sentencing, I started to believe the little man had a heart, at least where Duke was involved. But he proved me wrong. When they split, he never once promised Duke that he'd return after serving his sentence. After a year passed, he never returned to see Duke. At that point, I was certain the man had no brains or heart. I found he cared only for himself and really didn't care for Duke. If I were Lou, I would have come back. Betsy thought otherwise. She believed Lou had given Duke all of what little hope they shared—whatever that meant. I'm still working on Lazarus. Regardless, despite the joke of a fool, law and order prevailed in Greens Point, and the integrity and virtues of our peaceful country town shone brightly along the Ohio. All of the time and effort I put into writing this chronicle of events paid off. Greens Point stands tall on the pages of history.

✳ ✳ ✳

"The only town in the *entire* United States that boasts two—not one—two statues of Civil War heroes from the South and North, both from Little Egypt," barked the tour guide. He was dressed up in antique South: straw hat with a red-and-white paisley band, white pressed shirt with loose sleeves, and red vest with blue buttons and trim. He stopped before the first white bronze statue, commonly called zinc, cleared his throat, and read from the plaque:

LIEUTENANT COLONEL THORNDIKE BROOKS
March 11, 1828–1893
Marion, Illinois
FREEDOM FIGHTER
PRIDE OF THE SOUTH

He ushered about a dozen tourists around to the second statue, stopped, cleared his throat, and read:

BRIDGADIER GENERAL GREEN BERRY RAUM
December 3, 1829–December 18, 1909
Golconda, Illinois
FREEDOM FIGHTER
PRIDE OF THE NORTH

He hooked his cane onto his elbow to take photographs of a young couple standing and smiling in front of the two war heroes.

"Onward to shopping or lunch, antiques or some good ole southern-fried catfish fresh from the Ohio," I heard the guide announce. He twirled his cane and pointed forward into town. Mumbles passed around the tourists. He led them onto Main Street, away from the old man sitting on a bench, unnoticed by all their eyes squinting upward into the midday sun shining directly down onto the statues and reflecting off the sheet of water, before the sheet ripped and the water dripped from the fountain.

As the small crowd passed me, I nodded a welcome on behalf of our town, looked across the end of Main Street, and saw Wally Davis sitting on the bench. Wally drew in a long breath of air and slowly eased out a ripple of a chuckle, but not a soul was near to hear.

www.ingramcontent.com/pod-product-compliance
Lightning Source LLC
Chambersburg PA
CBHW050405030726
47503CB00006B/2025